D0455494

FIC   Demetz, Hanna.

The journey from
Prague Street

$16.95

DATE		

STORAGE ✓ 0965

IV

JUL 9 1990

San Diego Public Library

© THE BAKER & TAYLOR CO.

THE JOURNEY
FROM PRAGUE STREET

THE
*J*OURNEY
FROM
*P*RAGUE
*S*TREET

HANA DEMETZ

3 1336 02414 0965

St. Martin's Press   New York

This is a work of fiction. Any references to historical events or to real locales are intended only to give the fiction a setting of historical reality. The characters and incidents are a product of the author's imagination and their resemblance, if any, to real-life counterparts is entirely coincidental.

THE JOURNEY FROM PRAGUE STREET. Copyright © 1990 by Hana Demetz. All rights reserved. Printed in the United States of America. No part of this book may be used or reproduced in any manner whatsoever without written permission except in the case of brief quotations embodied in critical articles or reviews. For information, address St. Martin's Press, 175 Fifth Avenue, New York, N.Y. 10010.

DESIGN BY GLEN M. EDELSTEIN

Library of Congress Cataloging-in-Publication Data

Demetz, Hana.
  The journey from Prague Street.
  I. Title.
PS3554.E465J68   1990   813'.54   89-24278
ISBN 0-312-03852-6

First Edition
10 9 8 7 6 5 4 3 2 1

For Ruth Hein

In the snowy mountains
there flows a stream so cold;
that one who drinks from it
never will grow old.

—German folk song

It is the natural condition
of the exile, putting down roots
in memory.

—Salman Rushdie, *Grimus*

*B*REAKING AND ENTERING. She would never have thought herself capable of it. She had, days before, carefully and unobtrusively listened to her daughters' casual mention of Daddy going away for the weekend. Then she had silently, shamefaced, plotted to get hold of the apartment keys. She had smirked, to herself, about the fact that even though there would be "entering" involved, there at least would be no "breaking," since she had the keys safely in her purse.

She had left the house without saying where she was going or when she would be back, which was not her custom. She parked her car in the well-remembered street (her older daughter had been born on the same block, twenty-two years ago), where graduate students still lived in two-family houses, where the landlords were still mostly absentee, coming over once a month to collect the rent. She noticed the car in front; guessed that they had probably taken the train. The porch steps needed painting. The glass in the entrance door had a crack. The inside stairs, covered with faded and dusty plush, creaked under her steps. What will you say if the people downstairs are home, she asked herself, her heart pounding loudly, if they hear you, if they ask—

But the house seemed silent, empty.

The key needed turning twice. She stood for a moment, staring inside, listening, then entered. Carefully closed the door behind herself. She didn't know exactly why she was doing this, why she had come, what she wanted to see. She was fifty years old. They had been divorced almost two years now. She had heard stories of enraged wives ramming their former husbands' cars, of slaps exchanged in the street. She had felt fury herself, but not now.

She noted with interest that the living room was quite messy, with cushions on the floor. The bed in the bedroom unmade, dirty dishes in the kitchen sink. Paul's clothes hung neatly. Jennifer's were strewn on the floor; Jennifer was her older daughter's age. She resisted the impulse to pick them up. She checked out the bookshelf made of pine boards and bricks, student fashion, and pulled out a small volume. It was a collection of letters by Hilda Doolittle, the poet H.D., translated years ago by Paul and herself. She put it in her handbag. Then she spat on the dining room table.

She carefully turned the key twice again, carefully made her way down again over the faded and dusty plush. Outside, the bright sunshine surprised her. She had expected it to be dark already.

——

I HAVE HAD TOO MANY LIVES. Sometimes my past overwhelms me. The many layers often merge and make me feel disoriented. There is no chronology. Events overlap, reference points disappear, people who belong to one life suddenly appear out of context, in another.

But recently, there is a change. Recently, there is this need, this urge, to put things in order, to leave nothing entangled, unexplored, unresolved. The need makes me straighten drawers, weed out closets, finish quilting the patchwork quilts unknown American women started a long time ago. The simple symmetry of a sampler, with my named added at the bottom and the year, calms me, pleases me. I have managed, silently mocking myself, to arrange my books in my shelves, in alphabetical order. And for months now I have diligently listed, in a small notebook I bought for this specific purpose, every book I read.

All this probably has something to do with the fact that I will be sixty this summer, a fact that amazes me, for I still get ecstatic driving fast, with the roof down. A Mozart sonata on the stereo, even Neil Diamond on the radio, still "send" me, as my daughters would say. I suspect that the neatened drawers, the finished quilts, the books arranged according to author, they all serve a purpose. They protect me, they make me feel that I can cope with chaos, with the many layers, with the memories of many places: Moravia, Prague, Cambridge, Lisbon. By making external order, I try to put an outline to the many lives of my past. There still is no chronology, but at least they are contained, they no longer threaten to spill one over the other. I can take them out, singly, and put them back again.

There is, of course, another reason for this need for external order. It has to do with my living with Bernard. Bernard is blind, and any thing that is not in its place, a book forgotten under a chair, the newspaper not in its usual spot, a half-emptied grocery bag left on the kitchen floor, will puzzle him, even make him stumble. I used to wait for angry outbursts in the beginning, holding my breath: I had, for thirty years, lived with Paul, who would lose his temper at the slightest irregularity, the smallest mishap. But Bernard, I found, is blessed with an almost angelic patience. And, at one very precise moment it was that patient good nature that convinced me to marry him: when his Seeing Eye dog, confused and made playful by my new presence, forgot to move out of the way and Bernard, losing his balance, crashed to the floor. There he sat, laughing, with the huge black Labrador, terribly upset, poking him with his paw. That was seven years ago.

At that time I was still living in Cambridge, still smarting from the divorce. My fall, if you want to call it that, had been swift and spectacular: one day I was the generally respected wife of a senior member of the department, a sought-after hostess, a pillar of society, and the next—

But no, it didn't happen that fast. It is only my memory compressing the contrast.

But a contrast there certainly was. I had to start looking for a job, because the teaching position I had held for twenty years, five hours a week, would not feed me, and I could not stand the thought of grudgingly offered handouts from Paul, who had dropped me with such haste. I took typing tests ("Oh dear, only thirty-eight words per minute," said the girl in personnel, "and two typos!") and found that the world had changed since I had last worked in an office. Also, I was much too old for the lowly jobs I could apply for. I was forty-eight. It took a small scene, which I staged in the personnel director's office ("Look, I have worked for this university for a quarter century, don't tell me now that I'm unemployable!" I shouted), to get me a job as secretary. The large white house in the suburbs, which Paul had so coveted and which I had never really liked, was sold. The ultimate irony of the situation only became clear to me many years later. Although the divorce had been Paul's idea, although it had been his wish to change his life, it was ultimately my life that, again, had been turned upside down, inside out.

———

AN AUTUMN SUNDAY, NOON. Gently, the sunlight filtered through the old elm. The leaves had not yet begun to turn. Behind the large white house, the apple tree sheltered promises of glowing red. They were having lunch in their kitchen: sardines on toast, with mayonnaise and lemon juice, and white wine left over from last night. How pleasant this is, Helene thought, this silence filled with sunlight, now that the girls have their own lives. There were so many years of Sunday-morning rush and chaos. This is iridescent, calm. The new school year is beginning. I will forget the bad summer. There have been bad moments before, many times, and I have been able to forget them. I will go on and be happy. I have many reasons to be.

Earlier that morning she had watched Paul shaving, and they had considered whether they could afford a trip at Christmas. "We could send the girls skiing," she had said, looking at him in the bathroom mirror, "and go to the theater every night." Paul was very handsome, even when his cheeks were white with lather he was very handsome, almost unchanged after thirty years, except for a few wrinkles around his eyes, with a flamboyant shock of dark hair. She still liked to watch him shave. She gently felt for the small bald spot on the back of his

head, a leftover from his fall down the stairs a month
ago. It was almost overgrown now.

Later, they were having lunch. A lawn mower next
door suddenly began to rattle into the silence. "These
Americans," she said and laughed. "They certainly don't
observe Sunday, do they? Such an infernal racket at
lunchtime!" She got up to close the kitchen door, sat
down again and picked up a piece of toast.

Paul looked at her quickly between a bite of sardine
salad and a sip of white wine. "We ought to be talking
about existential things," he said.

Helene looked up, surprised. "Why?" she said,
chewing. "Can't you get away at Christmas?"

"I intend to change my life," he said.

She looked at him. She had a piece of toast in her
mouth, forgot to swallow. The kitchen clock above their
heads made a deep humming sound. She swallowed.
"What—how do you mean?" she said and shook her head.

"I'm not going to wait," he said, "until they carry me
out of here feet first, one fine day."

She looked at him. She wanted to say something,
but her voice did not seem to want to come out. "What
are you going to do?" she finally whispered.

He took a sip of wine. Carefully he set down the
glass. "Maybe we will have to consider divorce," he said.

The clock hummed. Their neighbor walked past the
kitchen door with his lawn mower. For a minute the
noise permeated everything.

"I see," she said. "I see. Divorce. Just like that."
Suddenly, unexpectedly, she felt her cheeks turning red,

felt her temples turning red, and her ears, and then the red creeping under the roots of her hair. Shame welled up, her heart was beating hard now, harder than the lawn mower next door, terrible shame at not having suggested it herself, years ago. Shame, terrible shame at being had. "All right," she said. "All right. Why not? If that's how you feel, why go on living here?"

She got up, replaced the chair carefully without hurting the basset hound lying under it, and walked over to the window. She registered that it was not Jack who was mowing the lawn but Mike, his son. He had tied a blue bandanna around his forehead to keep his long hair out of his face, and he waved to her. She raised her hand.

Paul, behind her, said, suddenly uncertain, "Maybe we should talk some more?"

She quickly turned away from the window. Her anger was now everywhere, hammering in her head, in her shaking fingertips, in her shaking knees. Anger, sown over many years and never harvested, anger at cringing for so long under his temper tantrums, now bursting forth with a force that she could not halt, that she herself could barely comprehend. She walked over to the table, collected the plates and the silverware, resting her fingers on them. She began rinsing the plates. "What is there to talk about?" she said over the warm faucet. "You seem to have made up your mind already. What am I supposed to say now?"

She had stacked the plates and the silverware, and wiped the kitchen counter. He hesitated in the middle of the kitchen. He said, "You could move to Europe."

She halted, the dishrag in her hand. She shook her head. "To Europe? What would I move to Europe for? We have two American children, don't we?"

He shrugged and left the kitchen. He went up the stairs; the couch in his study creaked. He had lain down for his nap, as he always did on Sunday afternoon.

The lawn mower rattled past the kitchen door once more. Then it moved away, was turned off. In the sudden reverberating quiet, sunlight shimmered on the elm leaves.

———

*B*ERNARD, THEN, IS THE TOP LAYER, the benevolent daily presence. We met because he was curious and persistent, traits that are not, I am told, typical for someone with his handicap. He had read (oh yes, he reads, with the help of ungainly machinery, which sits on top of his desk, enlarging and projecting words onto a screen), he had read a review of my book, and had ordered the book from his bookstore. And then he wrote (oh yes, he writes, with the help of the same beautiful invention), then he wrote me a fan letter. At that time I was getting a lot of fan letters.

My book, my English translation of my book that had been published ten years before in German, the story of the destruction of my family, had hit American bookstores at the right time. The labor of translating, which had been an act of pure self-preservation after the divorce, since it had kept me from gritting my teeth in helpless rage and from tearing my hair in deep sorrow, turned out to have been beneficial in every way. Suddenly I was, in a modest way and for an instant, a minor celebrity. There were reviews, full-page ads, columns in *Newsweek*, a discussion on public television, and phone interviews with Herbert Mitgang and George Will. There were many fan letters, and I dutifully answered each one of them: "Thank you for your kind words about my novel. It is for readers like you," etc.

But Bernard did not intend to let me stop there. He wrote back. And he wrote again. I was at first intrigued by this persistent blind man who wrote funny long letters, signing them, "Me and Dog." Then I turned peevish. I was, after all, still a celebrity and did not have time to answer letters, which kept arriving every week. But Bernard was not one to give up. "That's quite all right with me," he wrote. "I can write enough for the three of us." Which he did. Although his persistence annoyed me, his letters kept me laughing. Then he began sending flowers, whole basketfuls of them. Never before had I received so many flowers. I had to relent, thank him. Soon he announced that he had booked a flight to Cambridge, because he was determined to meet me. Could I be at the airport, since his dog didn't know his way around Massachusetts?

I was, at that point, impressed by his spirit. I bought a new dress and went to the airport. What I saw there, stepping from the flimsy commuter plane, was a tall man with beautiful hands and a face not unlike that of Leslie Howard. Love at first sight, at fifty-three? Yes, love and sympathy and affection at first sight.

———

THE GIRL SHE ONCE WAS, a lifetime ago, in Prague: pale and thin, her hair tied into a small knot at the nape, her long arms in a pale blue sweater of recycled wool. The New Look had prescribed the length of her skirt, thirty centimeters from the floor, no more and no less, and the last remaining linen sheet from her mother's once immense trousseau had been utilized. The heavy linen, dyed navy, could almost pass for lightweight English tweed. Two camel's-hair blankets, dyed navy, had been fashioned into a coat. Navy, she remembered, had been the color for young girls from a good family, before the war. The family was no more, she knew, but this way she could pretend. The family had been lost in many transports, had been gassed, had died of broken hearts, of crushed hopes, had been detained, were dead of exhaustion. Only the girl she once was had been left. She was alone.

She lived by herself in a small apartment in an apartment house at the edge of the city: a hallway, a bath, a living room and a tiny kitchen; they called it a studio. After the end of the war, when it finally became clear to her that nobody would come back, that her whole family was dead, the girl had exchanged the large apartment of her parents for the studio on the fourth floor. The young couple who had owned the studio had been very eager to get the large apartment. They were expecting a baby. So they had simply moved without the Housing Ministry's permission: they did not want to apply for months and tie themselves up in all the red tape, only to be told at the end that they could not move to begin with. The young couple had bribed the superintendent, and they exchanged apartments, hoping that the other tenants would keep quiet about it. They did.

The girl had filled the studio with all the furniture she had been attached to: the couch, covered in brown velour, the two armchairs with a lamp table, the bench to hold her gramophone and her collection of Mozart records, the armoire, the small table. She was proud of her invention, a long board on top of the radiator, where she arranged books and flowerpots and Gerd's photograph in a wooden heart frame. Nobody would have guessed that the long board was not really a shelf, that it was part of her parents' double bed.

The girl had not kept the Oriental rugs; they seemed too middle-class, too much a symbol of what had been destroyed. She had taken only a beige-and-brown wool rug with her to the fourth floor. The superintendent put the Orientals in the storage room. From time to time he would stop Helene in the front lobby to report that he was putting mothballs on the rugs, she would be grateful to him one day. She always thanked him dutifully. She had been brought up to be very polite, and she had learned that agreeing to things as they came to her would protect her from more sorrow.

The studio was very comfortable with the large window, which she did not have to cover, since there were no more blackouts. She had put a ruffle of flowered fabric, made from her mother's old robe, on top of the window. There were only meadows underneath, and then far away the houses on the hills of the Weinberg section. Paul, later, would call the view at night the "Manhattan skyline."

Helene had met Paul in that first postwar summer, during one of Anne's visits. Anne's father had not returned from Auschwitz, either. Her mother was in northern Bohemia, waiting to be sent to Germany, because she was German and all Germans were being sent there. Anne didn't know whether she should let them send her to Germany, as well, or whether she should stay: she was half Jewish, just like Helene, and had the choice. But whereas Helene was equally fluent in Czech and German, Anne had not learned any Czech and would have difficulty registering at the university. She didn't really know what there would be for her to do in Prague, where no German was allowed to be spoken now. So she waited, undecided, suspended. In the meantime, Prague was quite pleasant. There certainly was more food than in Germany. One really knew almost nothing about conditions in Germany, except that things were terribly devastated. It was as if the country had ceased to exist.

Anne knew many men. Wherever she went, she met new ones; Helene, who was reticent and often shy, sometimes envied her that ability. Anne had known Paul for a long time, she had met him during the war. In those days Paul had worked in a bookstore, and Anne had gone there often because she found him very handsome and very intelligent. In the final autumn of the war he was also picked up and sent to a camp: someone had reported that he had made a disparaging political remark. He had come back in the summer and Anne, in Prague for a visit, invited him for dinner to Helene's studio. She had brought a bagful of cauliflower and a bagful of potatoes from northern Bohemia with her, and one usually shared what food there was.

Paul arrived with a bouquet. He really was handsome, with curly dark hair, tall and bony. It was clear after the first half hour that he was not at all interested in Anne. He watched Helene, who was silent, and told her, "Why don't you give me a call when you're free?"

Helene was not free. She spent her every evening, her every weekend, lying on the brown velour couch, staring at the photograph in the wooden heart frame. She didn't call Paul until much later that fall.

———

YEARS LATER, at the time of Paul's first sabbatical, they drive through Germany. The backseat of their Morris Minor is playroom and sleeping quarters for Elizabeth, who is not quite two. Elizabeth has Paul's dark curls and Helene's blue eyes, and she likes having her two grown-ups at arm's reach for hours on end. That morning they had left the spotlessly blue-and-white German town, where the blue-and-white ship that had brought them from New York seemed to lie at anchor directly in the green meadows, where proud and well-fed cows marched along the quays. At lunchtime they stop at a country inn and eat at an oak table under tall chestnut trees. Everything is neat and well-ordered: the large farms, the villages with freshly painted houses, the patchworks of deep-green meadows and yellow wheat fields. Only the towns still show, fourteen years later, traces of war. A new and modern hotel is built into the ruins of the old, the new upper stories of a house sit on a lower floor that survived, a graceful old archway is supported by newly set stonework.

After dinner they take a walk around the town square, with Elizabeth pulling them toward the lighted shop window of a toy store. Holding Elizabeth's hand and exclaiming with her over the animal pull-toys and wooden dolls with yellow pigtails, Helene stares. Almost hidden behind a cart filled with Steiff animals is a wooden frame shaped like a heart.

———

WHEN ANNE CAME TO PRAGUE for her next visit, she asked, "Are you going to give Paul a call?"

"Yes," Helene said. "I will give him a call."

"But Helenka," Anne said, bemused, "you won't know how to cope with two men at once! I mean—what about Gerd? Some day they are going to release him—"

Helene went to the window and picked up the photograph in its wooden heart frame. "I know," she said, studying it. "I know. I have thought about it a lot. Ever since the end of the war I have thought about it, ever since I've known that nobody came back from those camps, your father didn't either. And I don't think that I will ever be able to forgive Gerd—"

Anne shook her head, not understanding. "Forgive Gerd what?" she asked.

"Forgive him for being part of it," Helene said, sadly.

"But what could he do?" Anne cried. "What could he do? He was just a soldier—"

"I know," Helene said again. "He was just a soldier. It was easier when he was missing, when I thought that he had died, after the invasion, in France. As long as I thought that he had died, too, it didn't mean anything, the fact that he was a soldier, a German soldier. He was dead, just like everyone else, I didn't think about the two sides. But when his letter came—"

"That was amazing," Anne said, shaking her head again.

"Yes," said Helene, remembering the amazing day. "The mailman thought he was seeing things, a letter from America, from a prisoner of war! He was so perplexed about it that he forgot to denounce me to the police, for receiving a letter with the address written in German."

Helene smiled at the memory. Then she went to her dresser, opened the top drawer, and took out a bundle of letters. She smoothed the top one, which was unlike all the others, written on a single-folded blue sheet without an envelope, marked "Airgram" with a bright stamp. She sighed. "When this letter came, things were suddenly different, very different. Of course I was happy that he was alive, you know that. But there are all the horrible things standing between us now—"

"You'll forget about them," said Anne.

"I don't think I can," said Helene.

"So you haven't answered him?" Anne asked.

"No, I haven't answered him."

"And you are going to call Paul," said Anne.

"Yes," Helene nodded. They were both silent.

Then Helene said, "Come, Annie, I need your help. I cannot do this alone. I want to burn Gerd's letters. It is time."

"Helenka, listen to me," Anne said urgently. "Listen. You know that I'm not jealous or envious or anything. But Paul is not—he is not for you. He is a cold fish. Stay away from him."

"I have no one else," Helene said. "I am alone."

"That's what I mean," Anne said. "You are alone. He will have to be your friend, and your father, and your mother. He will have to be all that. And I don't know if he can do it. Write to Gerd, please."

"I can't," said Helene. "I can't."

She had already crushed several folded sheets of paper. Dropping them in the kitchen sink, she put a match to them. The flame flashed upward, performing a yellow dance, and went out. Gerd's handwriting crumbled, turned brown, disappeared. Anne watched silently as Helene crushed one letter after the other. She flushed the black ashes several times. Tears were running down her cheeks. The two young women did not look at each other.

Finally Anne spoke. "Paul," she said. "I've known him a lot longer than you have. Paul was in love with a girl, two years ago, before they locked him up. It was an unrequited love. He wrote poems to her. But she wouldn't have anything to do with him. Maybe she was a Nazi who didn't want to get involved with a half Jew, I don't know. And then, when he was in the labor camp, she was killed here in Prague, in the February air raid. Full blast, outside Saint Thomas's church."

Helene had burned all the letters now. "Did he find out about it in the camp?" she asked. She took Gerd's photograph out of its wooden heart frame, looked at it, smoothing it. Then she put a match to it, too. She threw the frame into the garbage pail.

Anne was watching Helene. "No," she said after a while. "They couldn't tell him about it till he came back, in May."

Helene folded her hands and was silent. She had stopped crying.

"I have to tell you what he did, what Paul did, Helene," Anne said. "After they had told him, he went to bed with Irma—you know, with his father's girl friend. She boasted about it afterwards." She shook her head. "That's what he is like."

Helene was silent.

"I don't know," Anne said. "I don't know if he will not hurt you. You are alone and I will be gone, too—"

Helene washed her hands and her face. Then she went to sit next to Anne and patted her cheek. "Poor Paul," she said. "So he has been hurt, too. He needs someone to love him."

———

BERNARD'S GREAT-GREAT-GRANDFATHER, when he was barely sixteen, had not only spunk but imagination. He left the ghetto in the small market town of Ichenhausen, in the Kingdom of Bavaria, secretly and by night, determined to go to America. I imagine he walked to Hamburg, for surely he did not have enough money to travel by stagecoach. Perhaps a compassionate peasant gave him a ride once in a while, perhaps they let him sleep in the barn when it rained. I sometimes imagine the young boy: surely there were moments when he was afraid, when he thought of turning back. Once in steerage (Did he pay for his passage? Did he hide for those three or four weeks it took, in 1800, to cross the Atlantic?), once in steerage there was, of course, no turning back. I like to think that he found a friend on board, maybe a family, who took care of him when he got seasick, when he was thirsty. What did they do when they first landed in Philadelphia? Did the family who took him under their wing have friends who told them what to do, how to speak? All I know is that the boy got himself a cart and began selling patent medicines from door to door, from street to street, from village to village. He did so well that he soon had money to send for his three brothers: they arrived from Ichenhausen, one every year, for three years. Soon they had a horse, another cart, another horse. The medicine bottles soon bore their name. They branched out, built their own distillery. The patent medicine was replaced by whisky, which in a way was also medicine; business boomed. The four brothers married, built houses, were instrumental in building the large synagogue in downtown Philadelphia. Their sons and their daughters became pillars of the Jewish community. When Bernard, the great-great-grandson, retired, because of his failing eyesight, in 1974, the family firm was producing, among other things, one of the best-known American candies. Ichenhausen, if remembered at all, was only an indistinct memory.

My own family's history is similar, up to a point. My great-great-grandfather also left the ghetto behind, and he also began by pulling a handcart along many dusty country roads. His son also bought horses and made the business flourish. His grandson also thought of the fame and welfare of the town that had become their home. There was only one fateful difference. My great-great-grandfather, instead of aiming for America, only walked north from Prague, toward the mountains and woods dividing Bohemia from Saxony. And this small difference, this lack of geographical premonition, one hundred and forty years later would mean that my family ceased to exist.

———

*T*HEY SPENT A LOT OF TIME in the studio, on the brown velour couch. Helene was a diligent pupil, and Paul an enthusiastic teacher. He came to visit almost every night (he had enrolled at the university, with a concentration in English literature). Sometimes, when he was late, Helene waited up for him: she had exchanged two of her mother's bath towels for a half pound of Lyon's tea, and it pleased her to serve the tea to Paul in her mother's pretty blue tea set. At other times she was already asleep because she had to get up early for her job in an art shop. She colored black-and-white prints depicting the village of Lidice, which the Germans had destroyed as a reprisal during the war. The prints she had colored were "selling like hotcakes," the owner of the art shop told Helene every day.

Helene had established an assembly-line method applying the watercolors. One hour was all she needed to finish ten pictures. Only the cloudy sky sometimes presented difficulties. But the owner of the art shop was not especially fussy, and the sky really did not have to be the same every time. When she was asleep Paul would wake her, his hands and his face cold from the winter night.

On Sunday afternoons, happily tired and hungry, they would venture out to the Flora Restaurant on Weinberg Hill, where you could get canned cherries without coupons to top off the obligatory potatoes and gravy. Potatoes and gravy were what most restaurants served, and one didn't ask too many questions about the gravy's ingredients.

Helene admired Paul. She liked his easy way of talking, his ability to see humor in the absurd situations that were happening all around them. Very often a single word or a gesture would bring back to them memories they had in common. They had both grown up with Czech as well as with German, had even spent early wartime vacations in the same summer resort.

One Sunday afternoon they sang to each other. Paul taught Helene Kurt Weill's song about Mack the Knife, which he thought amusing. Helene sang her favorite folk song, the one about the snowy mountains where the cold brook flows. When she had finished the fourth stanza, about the lover who remained ever young and would not return to his sweetheart, she grew sad.

Paul kissed her. He said, "I will never be like that. Even when we're old, I'll always come back to you."

He told her about his parents and he made his tale sound comical, made himself sound like a bystander, cool and unconcerned. His father, an actor, had always been susceptible to the charms of young actresses. There had always been scenes at home, screaming, reconciliations, more scenes. There never was enough money; sometimes his mother had to take in sewing. When Paul was thirteen, his parents divorced, and his mother married one of her rich admirers. Paul was shuttled between and fought over by his parents until the beginning of the war. Then his stepfather abandoned his mother and him, left them in a large house in the suburbs, and fled to England. The house was confiscated by the Germans, and Paul's mother was deported. She died in the Ravensbrück concentration camp. Paul could stay behind because he was only half Jewish, living with his father until the last wartime summer, when he was twenty-one. Then someone reported him for an anti-Nazi remark, and he was arrested and sent away. He spent several weeks in custody in Auschwitz, then was released into a work camp in Bohemia. He made even that sound like a farce, describing how his father had bribed the Nazi judge with a Christmas goose. After his release at the end of the war he went back to live with his father, whom he didn't like.

She admired him, but she sensed the anger behind his jokes. That's why he is the way he is, she thought, that's what Anne was talking about. We have both been hurt, and I will be kind to him. He needs me much more than Gerd would have needed me. Gerd was strong.

They often went dancing, Helene loved to dance. During the war there had been dancing only at private parties, secretly, and in the last war year it had been strictly forbidden. Now big bands were playing everywhere. Walking at night along Wenceslas Square you could hear them from every café and every nightclub, snatches of the new songs that the Americans had brought with them, "Gonna take a sentimental journey," and "In my solitude." Everyone was learning the lyrics by heart.

Some girls who spent weekends in Pilsen, where the Americans had halted, reported that the bands were even better there. Anne, who went to Pilsen often, reported that the Americans' way of dancing the jitterbug was unbelievably graceful, not clumsy like the attempts of the Czech boys. She also said that the way American uniforms were cut was out of this world. Anne was now looking forward to going to the U.S. zone in Germany, just for the pleasure of seeing more of the American uniforms.

———

*F*OUR YEARS LATER, after Helene and Paul had escaped from Czechoslovakia and had become Displaced Persons, the Bavarian border police handed them over to the Americans. The C.I.C. thought their backgrounds interesting enough to keep them for a week of questioning in a remote villa. That turned out to be a week of surprising luxuries. In the nights, their subconscious had not yet registered that they were beyond danger: they woke up regularly, shaking and clutching one another. Their nightmares were of being back in Prague, unable to get out, being lost.

But every morning an American breakfast, consisting of bacon and powdered eggs and canned orange juice, was brought to their room. At noon they were picked up by a jeep and driven to a military compound, where they were fed American army rations on metal trays, in an American mess hall. They had never eaten such good food. Helene became addicted to canned pineapple. She dreamed, ate, drank, smelled canned pineapple, became obsessed with the sun-yellow rings. And the mess-hall cooks put double and triple portions of them on their trays, and Helene ate them all.

One day, as they waited their turn at the mess-hall door, the only civilians in sight, a large column of new

Sherman tanks came rolling by. They were things of terrible beauty as they approached one after the other: taller than the Quonset mess hall, gleaming, rattling, the white stars and the writings on their sides messages from another world. The ground trembled as they passed.

They stood there motionless, gaping. Never before had they seen anything as grand, as powerful. "They must be classified top secret," Paul whispered to her, "and here we are, staring at them—" He did not finish, for they saw an officer jumping off one of the giants, loose-jointed, heading toward them. Helene grabbed Paul's hand. They had just come from a country where an approaching uniform had always meant only one thing: danger. People went to prison in Czechoslovakia for much lesser crimes than looking at tanks.

But the officer, when he reached them, saluted and said, smiling, "Will you kindly step inside?" He opened the door of the mess hall for them, before he ran back to catch up with his clanking, olive-green proof of American military superiority.

When eventually they contemplated the country where they would want to spend their lives (they were certain about wanting to spend them together), it was this encounter with the relaxed generosity of Americans that made them apply for immigrants' visas to the United States.

———

*T*WO YEARS AFTER THE DIVORCE, as an act of defiance against my age and my newly poor status, I had bought a bright red MG. This not only impressed Margaret, who was then fourteen and greatly obstreperous, but also added to my being a statistic: divorcées, the studies showed, shortly after the divorce are apt to acquire (a) new lovers, (b) new wardrobes, (c) new cars. According to the statistics I was, due to my age, more a Displaced Homemaker than a Divorcée. But since I had never considered myself solely a homemaker, and since Paul began to be seen around town with girls not much older than his daughter Elizabeth, I felt that my displacement was of a different kind. The bright red MG soothed my rage about being a Displaced Older Woman.

The MG turned out to be a small problem when Bernard arrived for the first visit, for the black Labrador Seeing Eye dog was much too large to be squeezed into the tiny luggage space behind the seats. But Bernard knew not only the location of every good restaurant in Cambridge but also the locations of car-rental agencies. "Blind people have to do a lot of research," he said, smiling down at me. I found that it took physical effort to keep myself from staring at him, touching him.

The weekend was very lovely and romantic, with

one very chaste kiss on the shores of the Charles River, and several less chaste kisses at the airport, before his departure. I was leaving for my summer job in Munich the following week and wanted to think things through. As it turned out, I spent the four summer weeks, when not working, writing to him or thinking about him. The simple act of buying a present to be sent to him for his birthday had me shaking in the men's department of Hertie's in the Kaufingerstrasse, alternating between hot and cold.

For Bernard, there seemed to be no question at all. He was going to marry me.

———

MEMORIES, scientists tell us, are formed in the hippocampus, a part of the temporal lobe that is believed to be involved in storing them. Some years ago, a California man, after an operation, suffered a sudden loss of blood to his brain. He survived, but lost his ability to remember. After he died several years later, scientists who studied his brain found that his total amnesia had been caused by a tiny lesion, which had formed during the few minutes of blood loss, in his hippocampus.

How many tiny lesions do we all carry, undetected, in our bodies?

———

*T*HE SECOND POSTWAR SUMMER, Paul received a
fellowship for one semester's study at the University of
Zurich. At the time, Switzerland seemed like a paradise
to hungry Europeans, and it did not grant many visas to
foreign students. But Paul's father had connections and
knew whom to bribe.

Helene remained in Prague. She was worried.
There had been a currency reform in the new republic,
and her father's savings had been put into a blocked
account. From time to time, a bank official, convinced by
her smile and her blue eyes, would be amenable to
paying several hundred crowns out to her in the new
currency. But Helene could see that she would have to
give up her studies, that she would need a regular
income. Her pay for coloring the village of Lidice and the
occasional expressions of admiration from smitten bank
officials were not enough to cover her living expenses. In
the fall she applied for a job with the British Embassy.
She had studied English during the war, and spoke it
well. The British Embassy offered her a job as telephone
operator. The salary would pay the rent for the studio,
for the food available with coupons, and for an occasional
book or record. There wasn't much else to buy.

After Paul's return from Switzerland, unpacking his

suitcase, Helene found a love letter, not written by her. Paul, it turned out, had met a Swedish student in Zurich during the summer. Yes, he had slept with her a couple of times, he told Helene, but she meant little to him. The letter had been put into his suitcase without his knowledge.

Helene was shattered. It had never occurred to her to demand of Paul to be faithful, but it never occurred to her that he wouldn't be. Now she felt deceived and somehow unclean.

"I don't like the way you look when you cry," Paul said. "A red nose isn't becoming to you, you know."

Helene quickly turned around to hide her face.

"It didn't mean anything," Paul assured her. "I told you that it meant nothing at all."

Helene blew her nose.

"And even if it had meant something," Paul continued, kissing her, "you must never make me feel tied down. I couldn't stand that. We don't belong to each other. We are both free."

"I will remember," Helene whispered.

"And we will never lie to each other," Paul said. "No matter what we do, we will never lie."

"I will remember," Helene said.

The film version of Shaw's *Pygmalion* was playing in Prague cinemas that fall. When people didn't talk of the food shortages, they talked of Leslie Howard and Wendy Hiller. Helene had never seen anything as beautiful as Eliza in her satin ball gown, curtseying and saying "How do you do?"

In the spring, two years after the end of the war, there was more food available, although food coupons were still needed for everything. Because she was not yet nineteen, Helene still received youth rations, which included one orange per week and a quarter pound of chocolates every month: luxuries, which she happily shared with Paul.

Anne, who had left for the U.S. zone in Germany, had sent Helene a pair of nylons in a letter. The fact that the letter arrived (there was no regular mail service with any of the occupied zones), and that its contents were undamaged and not stolen, again seemed like a miracle. The nylons were so thin that Helene was scared to wear them: compared with the one pair of heavy dark stockings one was issued with the yearly clothing coupons, they seemed like a message from another world.

But once in a while, even in Prague, they could feel a whiff of things getting better, a sense of hope and change, even if they had to stand in line for hours to get to them. There was Louis Armstrong with his trumpet, singing with his bruised voice, in a nightclub off Wenceslas Square. There was the length of lace that Helene managed to buy without coupons one day, to sew to the hem of an old summer skirt, just like the New Look. There was a Paul Klee reproduction to buy and hang on her wall, a small volume of poems, a recording of "Rhapsody in Blue," played by the London Symphony Orchestra.

Paul spent the third postwar summer studying in Oxford. Helene enjoyed working in the telephone ex-

change: it was a job many of her friends envied, for
connections with the British were considered the height
of fashion. From her window she could see the red
tile-covered roofs of the Old Town. In the afternoons the
embassy custodian would bring her a cup of tea, Earl
Grey, and cucumber sandwiches from the embassy's P.X.
When the summer was over, she took the train to meet
Paul at the Marienbad border station.

Paul reported on an insignificant summer romance
between Oxford and London, nothing meaningful at all.
She forgave him, for she remembered that he must not
feel tied down, that they did not belong to each other.
Besides, she was much too happy about his return to
spoil it with unpleasant thoughts. Life seemed wonder-
ful. With the Scottish kilt he had brought for her, and
with his new English tweed jacket and his Burberry
raincoat, they were one of the most elegant couples, one
of the most talked-about couples in Prague. She was
proud of him, proud of herself belonging with him. She
successfully imitated his air of arrogant boredom, which
he had adopted in Oxford.

But then, as autumn turned to winter, Eva appeared in Paul and Helene's circle of friends. Eva was
passionate about the sonnets of John Donne, reading
them aloud at every party in her beautiful alto voice. She
lured Paul away from his seminars. Their relationship
lasted several winter weeks.

"Of course I don't love her," Paul told Helene. "It is
partly intellectual attraction. She is very sensitive in
literary matters. And partly it is a purely erotic thing."

"I don't mean anything to you?" Helene asked.

"Of course you mean a lot to me," Paul replied. "But you don't own me, we don't own each other."

"Then go and don't ever come back!" Helene cried out and threw a book at Paul.

"I cannot do that," Paul said. "I cannot do that, because we belong together." He had just discovered Herman Melville, and in *Pierre* he began to see a symbol of his own conflict. Young Pierre's hesitating between the young and innocent Lucy and the passionate dark Isabel was, to him, much like his own predicament.

Helene was not feeling well. The food rations had been cut again and they were not adequate for nineteen-year-olds. There were no more oranges and no more chocolates. Czechoslovakia had had to reject the Marshall Plan on Stalin's orders, and the food supply that winter was even worse than it had been during the war. There was no one who would have supplemented Helene's diet with black-market supplies, and she herself was much too distressed to think about exchanging pieces of her mother's trousseau for food.

But then came a time when political upheavals pushed all personal grief into the background. In February all the democratic cabinet members resigned from the government, in protest over the Communists' actions. And the Communists, supported by the quickly commandeered trade unions and workers' militias, took over the country in a bloodless coup. Only several hundred students staged a protest march and were hit and spat upon. Stalin's emissary, Zorin, quickly arrived for a friendly visit. On the country's southern border, in Austria, the Red Army was staging maneuvers.

Helene was ordered to appear at police headquarters and instructed to report on all persons who had business dealings with the British. "We will show them, those damn Western agitators," the policeman told her.

Paul was called in by the Communist Students' Council, where they warned him that he could not hope for a university career, not even for a modest translator's job, unless he became a party member.

Their friends began to leave Prague, escaping to the West. Paul's friend Thomas took his skis and went for a winter vacation in southern Bohemia; he did not return. Another group of friends left for a weekend near the Bavarian border. They planned to jump off a train in a convenient spot somewhere, and ask for political asylum in Bavaria. Rumors about possible escape routes were everywhere.

Rumors were everywhere. Some people were convinced that the Western allies would not tolerate what was happening to the county, and would come marching in any day. "The Americans know the way. They were here three years ago," they said. Others tried to accommodate themselves to the new situation. "We've managed during the war, we'll manage now," they said, "Communists or Nazis, what difference does it make?"

In the spring it became evident that the new government had committed political murder in order to dispose of Jan Masaryk, the popular Minister of Foreign Affairs. The atmosphere became more and more suffocating. People were arrested in the middle of the night, just as in wartime, and not heard from for weeks. Sometimes they were released, without a hearing, without an explanation. Sometimes they were not.

Helene had made up her mind not to collaborate with the new masters. I should leave, she thought, soon. It will not take them long to catch up with the fact that I am not reporting to them. I should not be waiting for Paul.

But one day in April Paul came to see her at the telephone exchange. "It's all over with Eva," he told her. "Thank you for giving me enough time." He reached out for her and they kissed, ignoring the lights on the switchboard that flashed, announcing incoming calls. They decided that they would leave Czechoslovakia together as soon as possible. Leaving, they knew, would not be simple.

It was unthinkable that they would be able to depart legally: the borders had been closed off in the past few weeks, and only reliable Communist functionaries could hope for passports. To get to West Germany across the green border, walking through the vast Bohemian Forest, still uncharted and untouched, they would need a guide. A guide could lead them past the mine fields, through the uninhabited and closely watched villages of the border region. A name was whispered, an address that turned out to be false; however, it might lead to yet another address, to yet another name. That name again might prove to be false, a wild-goose chase, thank heaven it was only that and no informer behind it. And when one would, at long last, hit upon a real connection, there still was no guarantee that someone somewhere down the line might not take off with the agreed payment.

Paul and Helene spent the whole summer searching for a way out. Not until October did they hit upon a connection that sounded fairly dependable and would lead them into Bavaria. On a certain Saturday night the guide was to meet them in a certain mountain shelter in the vicinity of Dreisessel Mountain. On Sunday morning, early, he would take them across.

Helene sold some of her things, secretly, so that the neighbors would not learn about her plans to leave. She exchanged her mother's silver for a diamond, which she sewed into her underwear. She exchanged all the money she had for black-market dollars. Every one of her actions would have been enough to land her in prison.

On Saturday they said good-bye to Prague and took the train to the border station, pretending to be weekending tourists. The mountain shelter, which they reached at nightfall after a hard hike, belonged to an old man who was afraid of the city people. They, in turn, were afraid of him. The promised connection appeared neither Saturday night nor on Sunday. The old man only shrugged, he knew nothing, did not want to know anything.

On Monday morning they returned to Prague. Helene went from the train directly to the telephone exchange, still wearing mountain boots and ski pants. Paul deposited his rucksack at the station and went to the university, to attend his usual morning class on the Romantic poets.

Then life in the empty apartment turned into a bad dream: one week after the ghostly excursion to the border region, Paul met Christine. She was a fellow student who had been arrested right after the coup in February, had spent six months in prison, and was abruptly released one day, without a trial, without explanation, the way it was often done. In the English Department they whispered that in exchange for her release she had to promise to supply information to the Secret Police.

Paul began to neglect Helene again. First there were excuses and apologies, later confessions and confrontations. In the end, there were only silences. At Christmastime, Paul informed Helene that he was marrying Christine.

It was a lonely, gray winter. Helene managed to buy back the brown velour couch, and there she camped, with the "Manhattan skyline" outside her window. There were no connections to be found in wintertime: the snow lay high in the border regions, tracks were easily detected, nobody wanted to take undue risks. She moved between her studio and the telephone exchange as if in a daze, afraid when the door bell rang, afraid of a stranger smiling at her in the streetcar.

Only when the first flower women appeared in town with the first snowdrops did she begin to smile again. The memory of White Mountain was suddenly there: Gerd in his German uniform, pretending to blow the bugle. Burying her face in a bouquet of snowdrops, breathing the fragrance of earth, she felt that she would survive. She was used to giving up people who mattered, giving up things, used to making do with very little. The snow would be melting soon in the mountains. She would find someone to take her across.

But in March Paul rang Helene's door bell. The wedding date had been set, he said, but he could not marry Christine. He wanted to leave the country, and Christine did not seem to care about that at all; she had just ordered living room curtains for the new apartment, and her parents very pointedly discussed Paul's future career at Prague University. He was very distressed. "Help me," he said. "I belong with you."

"No," Helene said. "No. Not anymore."

Two weeks later Paul reappeared, with a bouquet of roses. He had canceled all the wedding plans, he said. He no longer loved Christine. Her family was much too overbearing, her aunts gossiped about him and gave Christine lace tablecloths for her trousseau, and doilies. Doilies! Could Helene imagine him living with doilies? Moreover, in Christine's face he could already detect that she would look exactly like her aunts, in twenty years. "You simply have to take me back, Helene," Paul pleaded. "I belong with you, we are good together, we understand each other, we always did. It was never as clear to me as now—"

"No," Helene said. "It is too late. Please take your roses back and go."

Two weeks later Christine came to Helene's door.

Her hair, which had been shaved in prison, had not quite grown back. She was very pale and very thin, ethereal. She said that Paul belonged to her now, even though he no longer wanted to get married. She was not willing to give him up. She knew the right people, people in the Party, she could guarantee him a fantastic future. The country was in need of dedicated people. One was expected to serve, self-denial was now required of everyone, Paul would learn that in due time. Helene, too, should participate in building a glorious future, work for progress instead of serving the imperialists and thinking of desertion—

This time I have a different role, Helene thought. I am the dark elusive Isabel, and she is the younger, innocent Lucy. And then she thought, with sudden clarity: Paul really needs me now, and I am committed to him, committed by my decision to love him. If he stays with Christine, he will be stuck here, and he will be lost. She will never let him go, and she will never leave here. I cannot let Paul be destroyed.

She stroked Christine's cropped hair, sadly and with compassion. She thanked her for her visit, for speaking so openly. After Christine left, she called Paul. She told him that she would forgive him, would flee with him. They did not belong to each other, but they belonged together, for better and for worse.

———

*T*HERE ARE IRONIES IN LIFE, coincidences, circles. The lesions that can cause memory loss break open
and, when not deadly, close again. New ones form. We
only know what we can see and feel, and with our limited
vision and scant understanding we try to make sense
of it.

———

*O*NE OF THE LETTERS that reached me after my
book about my family was published was a letter that
came from a rabbi of a congregation in a small town in
Pennsylvania. The rabbi wrote that his congregation had
acquired a Torah scroll from the small town of Přeštice in
Bohemia. He asked whether I could tell him something
about life there before the war. Since I was a child before
the war, I could not tell him much. But most important
for me was the fact that this particular Torah scroll had
come from the town that was the birthplace of my
mother's mother. She may have grown up worshiping

before this very scroll, she and her many brothers and sisters.

I was taken to Přeštice only once. My grandmother's maid, the Czech girl Mařka, also came from there, and on one of her vacations she took me to visit her own family and also the family of my grandmother. I was only five or six at the time, but I remember that I developed an ardent crush, in the course of one afternoon, on my grandmother's youngest brother. He must have been in his early fifties. I also remember waking up in red-and-white checkered featherbeds on Mařka's father's farm, with the rooster crowing outside and doves cooing, and the smell of chicory coffee coming from the kitchen.

There is further a memory of myself being taken by my handsome uncle, along with Mařka, to a Sabbath service. I had never attended a Sabbath service before: my mother had married a German, a law student, not altogether to her parents' liking. I was to be brought up a Czech like my mother, and a Catholic, like my father. A Jewish place of worship was as mysterious to me as the already sprouting Nazi sympathies of his own parents must have been to my father. I remember clutching Mařka's hand that time, for my handsome uncle had gone to sit downstairs, and peering through a curtain into a dark space below. There was a small group of men there, men who were chanting and crying, their black hats bobbing to and fro over their bent backs. Their cries and the darkness around them made me cry, too. I didn't know why they should be so mournful when everything outside seemed so fragrant and pretty. Hadn't I, just before, whispered to my handsome uncle that I loved him?

To quiet me down afterward, Mařka resolutely took me to church. There was gold and cherubs and light and heavenly music. In those long-ago and never-to-return days in prewar Bohemia, crossing religious boundaries was a simple thing.

And now, in Bernard's face, I sometimes detect a likeness, a similarity to my beloved uncle. There is, fifty-five years later and one whole continent away, the same quick smile, the same angle of shoulder, the same arch of eyebrow.

And the small town in Pennsylvania from which the rabbi's letter came is where Bernard's mother had grown up, many years ago.

———

*T*OWARD THE END OF APRIL of that year, the fourth year after the end of the war, Paul and Helene were married in city hall. Afterward they went for dinner to the best restaurant in town, spending all their money on food without coupons and for champagne, which was to be had under the counter. They danced to a band that successfully imitated Glenn Miller's orchestra. Nobody knew how long it would continue to play, before its members would be redirected into industry or the coal mines.

They continued searching for a connection who would take them across the border. They followed every lead, even traveled to remote villages where, someone said, there might be someone who could give them a tip. They could not find anything: the borders to the West were now almost hermetically sealed, and the chances of getting across without a guide who knew the terrain were very small. Rumors flew about people who had dared to set out on their own and were apprehended even before they could get to the border areas or were blown up by land mines.

At long last, in the fall, a connection materialized again. It was to lead to the border through the town that was Christine's home. They weighed their apprehensions against their desire to leave, and decided on the risk. This time it did not take too many preparations to be ready. The studio was empty of everything except the brown velour couch.

Sitting on their rucksacks in the overcrowded train, they discovered that Christine was in the next car. "She goes home every Friday night," Paul whispered, deathly pale. It was Friday night. Looking at each other, they refused to spell out the other possibility, the possibility that Christine could have been sent to watch them.

In Christine's town they got off. They were to meet their guide the following morning in the railroad-station hotel. After leaving the station, they hid in a dark corner and embraced passionately, for they were supposed to act the role of a couple of lovers on a clandestine weekend trip. Their connection in Prague had given them instructions about that. The Secret Police, he had told them, would thus be convinced that they were above suspicion. If they stop us, Helene thought, I will pretend to faint. They will be confused for a moment, and Paul can escape. Maybe.

Christine did not stop. She walked past without giving any sign that she knew them. She was a young student with cropped hair on her way home for the weekend, and that evening she had the power to send Paul and Helene to prison for many years. She soon disappeared into the mist of the October evening. Only her steps sounded, then it was quiet.

Early next morning their guide, a young man in a brown leather coat, really appeared. He greeted them with the password their connection in Prague had told them about. "*Moldau*," he whispered. They would, he then informed them, be driven closer to the border by a taxi, whose driver was also a member of the organization.

The taxi was a prewar Tatra, with tires that were smooth as black asphalt, and with springs winding through the upholstery. They drove through Christine's town, through the outskirts, past several villages. Then there were only houses scattered along the road, and barns in the meadows. Paul looked at their compass: they were driving west.

The driver was talking about a friend who had just

been sentenced to ten years in the uranium mines of Jáchymov. The boy in the brown leather coat said, "We will have to put his wife on our lists. She does not have a penny. And four kids."

"Hell," said the driver.

Again they drove through a village. In front of the tavern two parked motorcycles had license plates of the border police. Several village children were hanging around them. The boy in the brown leather coat turned, whistling through his teeth. Helene saw that the driver also was looking intently into his rearview mirror.

Three minutes later they saw a cloud of dust rising in the village behind them. The cloud moved; it was following them, growing larger. The driver stepped on the brakes. "Get out, quick!" he yelled.

"Let's go," said the boy as he opened his car door and jumped into the ditch, Paul after him, Helene last. The driver banged the doors shut, accelerating again, tires screeched—their rucksacks had remained in the front seat—dust and sand rose, Helene felt them penetrating her nose, her mouth, her eyes. The droning of the motorcycles was approaching—they pressed themselves into the ditch. There was a dark forest behind them. Now I know, Helene thought, why they warned us to wear dark clothes: we would be much more visible now—

The motorcycles raced past them, they did not slow down, did not stop, they drove past and away. Their droning hung over the ditch for a while, reverberating.

"Poor Karel," the boy said. "They'll catch him today for sure." He straightened, spat, wiped the dust and sweat from his face. "We have to get away quick."

They followed him out of the ditch, into the forest. The terrain went steeply uphill and they followed him, gasping for breath, catching on roots and branches. Only when it got dark did they slow down to rest. The boy took out his flashlight and showed them, on the map, the spot they had reached.

"It's fifteen kilometers to the border," he told them. "Over there are the mine fields. At night the patrols come through only every three hours, and they like to keep to the roads. That's what we have to keep away from. We'll go straight through."

He gave them each a piece of chocolate before starting out. The forest was thicker now. The boy walked through it securely. He knew every tree. Once they had to cross a service road: they stood still for minutes and listened. Helene noticed how the boy's brown leather coat squeaked with his every breath. It sounded dangerously loud in the night silence. Forty years later, she will still remember that sound.

When they had to cross an asphalt road, the boy motioned to them to take off their boots. "Every sound," he whispered, "carries for kilometers in the stillness. There is no point in taking the risk." All three of them hopped across the hardtop like children, one by one, clutching their boots to them. When they heard loud barking very close by, they froze. Only the boy calmly continued on his way. "Just stags," he whispered, turning to them. "Stags always make a lot of noise this time of year." A bit incredulous, they followed him, heaving sighs of relief. During the night they heard the barking often, sometimes far away, sometimes quite close. Again and again it startled them, terrified them. Forty years later, Helene will still remember that sound.

After midnight they reached the border. By flashlight the boy showed them his map again, and the spot on it that they had reached. They searched for the location on their own military map, and found it. Then the boy pointed out to them the direction in which they were to continue. "I have to go back," he said. "Karel also has a family, they will need me. You have to watch your compass very closely now. You could easily walk back into Bohemia from here. The trees are the same on both sides of the border."

Helene asked about border markers, but the boy smiled and told her that none existed in a primeval forest. He saluted them, turned around, and disappeared. A few twigs snapped for a while, that was all.

They continued in the direction he had shown them, but the border did not run straight at all. On their military map it twisted and turned like a peaceful meadow brook.

When the sky behind them began to lighten, they lay down, embraced for warmth, and slept. The pale October sun woke them when it stood above. They continued on their way, their clothes wet and torn, their limbs aching.

Only late in the afternoon did they hear voices in the distance. After they had crept closer, they found a group of woodcutters drinking coffee from thermos bottles. They were Bavarian voices, Bavarian woodcutters. Never before had a language sounded so beautiful to them.

———

OF COURSE THERE WERE DOUBTS. One doesn't marry, at fifty-three, totally doubtless, the way one did at twenty. Sobering thoughts popped up in the middle of the night. The basilisks and gargoyles decorating the turrets of university buildings smirked with special malevolence when I walked to my morning class: a bride, huh?

On one hand there was Bernard, attentive, who saw, without seeing, more than others, who wanted me to continue my life as it would have been had there been no war, no loss and no destruction. There was, after five rather improverished years, the world of elegant restaurants, weekends at country inns on the Delaware River, his bachelor apartment in Philadelphia, which a decorator had "done" almost exactly the way I had done mine after Margaret had left for college.

On the other hand, there were his three daughters, grown-up and on their own, but very much in evidence.

There was his former wife, who regularly called asking for his advice. There was the way people stared wherever we went, at the huge Labrador, at him, at me. And there were the concerns of my friends who had nursed me through the five postdivorce years. "He will want to run things, be in charge," Anne said, after she had come from Montreal to meet Bernard. "You are doing well on your own. Will you be able to let him be in charge?" And Sophie said, "He is handicapped, his life is poor compared with all that you can do. Won't he start resenting that?"

But then, finally, my twenty-four-year-old Elizabeth made the most sense of all. "But Mom," she cried, "all you have to do is love him!"

———

*T*HE BAVARIAN WOODCUTTERS BROUGHT Paul and Helene to the border police station, and after registering them as refugees, the border police handed them over to the Americans. One week later their life of luxury was over: a jeep took them to a refugee camp in Munich. There was no more pineapple, instead there were slimy noodles and red beets three times a day. The beets invariably dyed the noodles pink, no matter how much they tried to separate the two. In the dormitory there were goats and rabbits, which longtime Displaced Persons kept under the three-tiered army bunks. People sat on their suitcases all day, every day, talking politics. Watching for thieves, waiting. All of them were not quite sure what they were waiting for. There were not may visas to be had in those days.

Outside the camp gates, Munich was mountains of rubble, with passageways cleared in between for people to walk through. In front of a restaurant, people stood in line for a bowl of potato soup. Tin spoons were attached to the tables with chains. A blind man, dressed in what was formerly a German uniform, painfully felt his way to a stool and began eating with shaking hands. "Do you think he has someone to love him?" Helene whispered, watching, tears in her eyes. "I'm sure he does," said Paul. "The ratio here is four women to one man. Eat, this soup certainly tastes better than our pink noodles!"

Because they had no luggage, they were free to walk around: all they possessed they carried with them, the toothbrushes and toothpaste and the bar of soap the American soldiers had given them, the diamond in Helene's underwear, and the few dollar notes. They studied all the bulletin boards every day, and among the many notices searching for missing persons they discovered a request for English-speaking refugees, to teach small children in another camp. They applied.

The childrens' camp was deep in the Bavarian Alps, far from the mountains of rubble, far from the people waiting without much hope. It was a complete childrens' town, run by American refugee organizations, with schools, nurseries, kindergartens, and a fully equipped hospital. Helene and Paul were issued a room in the barracks, a room of their own, and next morning they began to teach reading, writing, and arithmetic. The children in their classrooms were war orphans of many nations, who would later be adopted by families in America and Australia.

By Christmas Helene and Paul had a tree, which they had cut themselves, decorated with paper stars, and a small red battery-operated radio they had bought on the installment plan. They had never seen red radios before, never seen radios that small, working entirely without electricity. American music came through from the American Forces Network, and whenever Helene's favorite, "Tennessee Waltz," was played, they would stop everything and dance. They felt rich and safe.

Helene had bought a piece of checkered fabric for their window, which framed an Alpine meadow. On clear days the craggy range of mountains above the meadow replaced the Prague "Manhattan skyline." The children in their classrooms brought them a young kitten, which they later christened Mathilda.

When summer came, they went on outings with the children and bathed in brooks underneath willow trees, which formed protective arches above them. On Sunday afternoons they would walk through the woods to a small café in the neighboring village, where poppy-seed cake was sold without coupons.

They turned an old kitchen table into a desk for Paul, and there he would sit every weekend, writing his first book. He would explain to Helene which research avenues he was planning to follow, and read to her the chapters he had finished. She was pleased when he praised her for asking questions, making suggestions. When he worked, she walked on tiptoe so as not to disturb him.

She had made her kitchen on the windowsill: there was an electric hotplate, and camp dishes made of tin. A net shopping bag was hung out the window, keeping meat and butter cool. Often a whole flock of sparrows would help themselves to snacks from the net shopping bag. Then the butter and the meat packages would carry tiny clean-cut traces of tiny sharp beaks.

But sometimes Helene did not quite succeed in making herself invisible. Then Paul would shout. He would suddenly become cold and strange, act as if she were an intruder, someone he barely knew. Once, when she could not stand his shouting any longer, she picked up a footstool and threw it at him. He jumped up and slapped her. Later he apologized and promised never to hit her again, Helene, deeply ashamed at having provoked him so, apologized, too.

OUR WEDDING TOOK PLACE in a synagogue, under a *chupah*, with five daughters and two sons-in-law in attendance. Bernard had cheerfully given up his apartment in Philadelphia and had moved his possessions to a condominium overlooking Cambridge's oldest park. Our furnishings blended as miraculously as our temperaments, with very few discordant notes.

He and the Labrador found Cambridge's layout easy to memorize: three blocks to the post office, five blocks to the barbershop, the newsstand across the park and to the right, around the corner. Sometimes the dog would misbehave: in the Italian bakery he would nonchalantly snitch a roll, hiding it in his maw, not biting into it until all witnesses were out of earshot. They became neighborhood fixtures: the huge black dog and his tall master, who would sometimes call out the names of the streets they were passing through, like a very efficient tour guide.

———

*T*HAT WINTER THEY LEFT the childrens' village in the Bavarian Alps and moved back to Munich. They began to work for a radio station that had just been organized to broadcast to countries behind the Iron Curtain. Paul, who had been hired to report on new literary developments in the West, was soon asked to take over the entire programming for the Czechoslovak section. He was a talented administrator, and he wrote with ease and extremely well. A whole crew of editors and secretaries and researchers was put at his disposal, most of them older than he. His essays, accompanied by Dave Brubeck's new cool jazz, were a huge success. Even hardened political commentators were often moved to listen in.

Helene was assigned to write a program for children, which went on the air every Sunday afternoon. Her experience in the childrens' village gave her a fresh and straightforward style. Sometimes her broadcasts were held up as examples of good radio writing.

They were proud of themselves. They wanted to do their share to change things for the better in Czechoslovakia, and they saw their chance in this work. They felt it was important for people at home to know what was going on in the West. They had no doubts that they would soon be returning home.

The German currency reform had wrought a transformation in Munich in the past year. Gone were the mountains of rubble, the town's center was beginning to be rebuilt. New shops, new restaurants were opening every month. Theaters were sold out every night, bookstores overflowed with new publications. Young people read their poetry in Schwabing cafés by candlelight, and a new singer, Gisela, belted out her songs of love and betrayal with a naughty Marlene Dietrich manner. Munich would become, everyone said, the new Paris of the fifties.

Paul and Helene had found a furnished room on the banks of the Isar River, where their landlady's maid

brought them tea in flowered Rosenthal cups every
night. On their way home from work they would buy cold
cuts and cheese, and many cans of pineapple for Helene.
They were earning good salaries, they had enough
money to buy food and, moreover, the food was free to
buy. There were no more coupons, no more rationing.
Only hot water was still scarce that winter, and their
landlady only allowed them one bath per person per
week. They scandalized the landlady and made the
young maid giggle, because they shared the bath every
time, thus managing to get two baths a week each.
Anne, who lived just around the corner in a building
whose hot-water pipe system had not been repaired yet
after the bombings, envied them this convenience. But
the lack of housing was still appalling, and she was lucky
to have a room, even if she had to use the public
bathhouse or heat water on the stove.

Anne was studying at Munich University, and she
and Helene saw each other often. They took long walks
through the English Garden, humming the French-
German song that had successfully crossed a border still
tightly sealed to travelers, "La vie en rose . . ." Together they laughed about Charlie Chaplin's *Monsieur
Verdoux*, wept over the young William Holden in *Sunset
Boulevard*, and dreamed of a time when they would be
allowed to travel freely all over Europe. They cajoled
Paul into taking them, dressed as two fiery Spanish
ladies, to the fancy-dress balls at the Hotel Palace.

In a garden restaurant that had just been rebuilt
where bomb craters had been, Anne took a sip of her

raspberry drink and said, "I need to ask you something, Helene."

Helene, who had been watching the fretted shadows of the linden trees on the white tabletop, looked up, surprised. "You sound so formal, suddenly," she said.

Anne took a deep breath. "I've wanted to ask you this for a long time. Why did you marry Paul?" she said, not looking at Helene.

"Why did I marry Paul?" Helene repeated. "But Annie, isn't it obvious? I married him because I love him. Why else?"

"Does he love you?" asked Anne.

Helene, about to answer in the same light manner, fell silent.

"For all the world," Anne said, serious, "for all the world you look like a happy pair, but I still want you to answer me. Does Paul love you?"

Helene's throat suddenly felt dry. She waved to the waiter and ordered another raspberry drink. Then she said, "I think he does—oh Annie, as much as he is capable of loving anyone—"

"Is that enough?" Anne asked quietly.

The waiter brought Helene's drink, setting it down on an oval tray. With appreciation he watched the two pretty young women, before he returned to his post under the new striped awning. Helene stirred, and drank. Then she sat upright, straightening her shoulders. "Annie," she said, "you worry too much. Paul is the most brilliant, the most amusing—"

"I know that," Anne said. "But does he love you?"

"I love him," said Helene. "We are married. We want to spend our lives together. He is fond of me, I know he is. What is there to worry about?"

"You," said Anne.

Helene poked Anne, playful again. "Come on now," she said. "Stop playing Cassandra. Smile at me."

"I don't want you to be hurt, that's all."

"I promise I won't be," said Helene.

They both fell silent. The edges of the leaf shadows moved over their bent heads. A tame dove, cooing, waddled over, looking for crumbs.

———

*T*WENTY-FIVE YEARS LATER, mercifully, Anne does not say "I told you so." She comes down from Montreal during spring vacation, old familiar Anne, who is now professor of English at McGill. They hadn't seen each other too often in recent years, but they only need to look at each other to pick up where they had left off the last time. The feeling that time and space really don't matter much is comforting to both of them.

That night Margaret, sensing the urgency of the visit, insists with twelve-year-old obstinacy on her customary chess game in front of the fireplace. Then she hangs around, ministering to the fire, watching the rain beating against the windows of the white house. It takes much reminding from Helene to make her tend to her own business. At long last she takes to her room, muttering, and they are alone.

———

MANY OF HELENE AND PAUL'S CO-WORKERS at the radio station were their old friends and colleagues from Prague. Even Eva was there, and her alto voice sounded romantic and beautiful on the air. But Paul was spending a lot of time with Yvonne, his assistant in programming. The plays of Anouilh and Christopher Fry and Sherwood Anderson were aired late at night.

After six months the radio station allotted them a furnished apartment. They enjoyed adding small personal touches to the standard billet furniture: an old print of Nieuw Amsterdam, which Paul had found at the flea market, an African violet in a pretty basket, a wall bookshelf to hold their growing collection of books. Mathilda, who had turned out to be a friendly tomcat, perched decoratively on a windowsill. Only when Helene placed several fat cushions on the floor to sit on did Paul have one of his sudden angry attacks. "This is not an artists' studio," he shouted. "I am an intellectual, not a bohemian!"

Helene quickly put the cushions back on the rented couch. She was surprised at the strength of Paul's objection. But she knew that his parents had lived a very unconventional life and felt his fear of slipping into the same pattern. She never put cushions on the floor again, and was careful never to act in a way that could be considered "artsy." She had enjoyed the costume balls they had gone to with Anne, but Paul was put off by this kind of social life; he no longer liked to dance. She gave up costume balls, gave up dancing.

Her passion for canned pineapple had abated now. There was enough food everywhere, and people in Munich were learning to choose from the amazing variety of it. The time that German sociologists later would call the clothing wave, the time of the early fifties when people reveled in buying clothing, was also coming to an end. Helene's closet now held a custom-made Harris tweed suit, an elegant navy suit that she had bought in Zurich, and a whole row of pretty dresses with bouffant petticoats. At a fashion show of a famous designer Paul had bought her a cocktail dress with an ankle-length skirt and a lovely heart-shaped neckline. Everyone thought it made her look like a *Vogue* model, and Paul was proud of her looking that way.

When Helene found that she was pregnant, there was no question in their minds that they were not ready to become parents. They were too involved with what they were doing, too unsure of where they would be spending their next years. Too strongly they felt, in the midst of their prosperity, their being displaced, homeless. But it was not easy to locate doctors willing to perform illegal abortions. Again, names were whispered, someone who had heard of someone would whisper a telephone number, which turned out to be disconnected, nonexistent. In a way it was almost hauntingly similar to their search for a connection four years ago: this time, again, the wild-goose chase, the fear of being denounced, the race with time.

Someone had given Helene a name of a clinic in a village east of Munich. When she arrived there by local train, she found a nightmarish place that prosperity had not yet reached, with manure heaps piled against house walls, mangy dogs snapping at her, snickering women peering at her from kitchen windows. They didn't know what a clinic was, had never heard of a doctor practicing anywhere near, she had better take the next train back, they didn't want strangers here, before they called the village Gendarm.

At long last, almost too late, there was a connection. The doctor told her to come to his office after hours and bring cash. She would have to come to his office alone and would have to hail a taxi afterward, but not any-where near his house. He would not use any anesthesia since that would entail risks, and she was not to scream, since that might betray them both to the neighbors.

Helene came alone and did not scream, and she walked the three blocks to a taxi stand afterward, holding onto house walls. Only days later, when the afterbirth gushed from her in bloody chunks, covering the bathroom floor, did she cry. Paul was gentle and considerate. He began spending more time with her than ever before, suggested beautiful weekend excursions to lakes in the mountains, and made plans for a long holiday in Sicily. She was moved by his attention. It seemed to her that their seven years of friendly familiarity and their shared past were enriched and made glowing by his warmth. Anne was wrong, she thought happily. Paul does love me, in his own way.

———

*M*Y MOTHER'S FALLING IN LOVE and marrying a poor German student must have been an act of defiance. I will never know, for she died when I was fifteen, long before we could have reached the time of open mother-daughter conversations, talks like the talks I can have with my daughters now. With her decision, my mother defied her family not on religious grounds, for to my grandfather, who considered himself a modern and enlightened man, as did many of his Central European contemporaries, Jewishness no longer meant commitment. He felt himself a Czech much more strongly than a Jew. (It was the Nazis who, later, taught him otherwise.) My mother, by marrying a German, must have dealt him a painful blow. But even more painful must have been the fact that she had spurned several eligible suitors, that she was marrying below her social class. My grandfather's family was not only well established in its

Czech milieu in the house on Prague Street, but also, due to hard work and foresight, financially very secure.

My grandfather was not one to flaunt his wealth: he lived modestly, walking to his office. Wenzel, the driver, did not do much driving; he spent his days polishing the ancient Škoda car, puttering on the grounds. When my grandfather's brothers arrived for visits, things were different: they arrived with liveried chauffeurs, with haughty maids attending to their even haughtier ladies, with conversations at the table endlessly revolving around "the market." I remember being scrutinized, through many lorgnons, as the product of their niece's misalliance; although by the time I was able to form these memories, my father could not have been a poor student anymore. He was by then a lawyer and their respectable equal.

Bernard's family, fifty years later, did not put lorgnons to their eyes when scrutinizing me. They accepted me, after only a moment's hesitation. And in their manner, in many of their gestures, in their conversations about business and "the market," I saw the ways of my own family preserved. Watching them, I could imagine that war, death, gas chambers, had never existed, that the world was the way it had been before. Most of all I saw that lost world in Bernard's old aunt Beatrice, who mournfully, in her kitchen, talked to the caterer about me. "Just imagine," she said, "the poor thing left her country without even taking her furniture!"

———

*T*HAT FALL PAUL AND HELENE were in a serious car accident. As they went home from the theater one night, their cab was rammed by a drunken driver. While Helene escaped with scratches and bruises, Paul, who had been sitting on the side of the impact, was thrown out of the car, against a curb. Helene, in her stocking feet, her face bleeding, ran around, looking for Paul. For a long time she could not find him. It was dark, and he had been flung an unbelievable distance. When she finally found him, moaning, with a small pool of blood under his head, she for some unfathomable reason looked up to the street sign above and was hit with another blow. The street was named after someone whose first name was Gerd.

For a week that seemed endless, Paul floated near death. He had a serious concussion, and his broken ribs had pierced one lung. Pneumonia set in. Several times Helene was called to the hospital in the middle of the night. Nuns, their long black habits covered by white nurses' aprons, knelt by Paul's door, praying.

It was a long time before the doctors lost their look of concern. It was three months before Paul had recuperated enough to return home. Very often he had violent headaches and became upset as soon as Helene left his side. She sat with him and read to him, cooked his favorite foods, and took him for walks in the blinking, glowing snow. That winter they talked a great deal about their future. Paul told her about his dissatisfaction, his impatience with what he was doing: his work for the radio station had become routine; it no longer interested him. "We will never go home again," he said one day. "Nothing will change, we will forever be exiles." He spoke about wanting to go back to school, wanting to study at an American university. They remembered the Americans' relaxed generosity, their easy acceptance.

When Paul was completely well again, in early spring, they applied for American visas. The quota for student visas was not nearly filled in those days, and several months later they received permission to emigrate. They found a home for Mathilda the tomcat, and packed their suitcases. From a military airport in northern Germany, a Flying Fortress, still bearing wartime camouflage, carried them westward.

Arriving at Idlewild Airport, after lengthy stopovers in Shannon, Ireland, and Gander, Newfoundland, they heard that Dwight Eisenhower had just been elected president. Election posters still hung everywhere. On the radio, Rosemary Clooney sang, "Come on-a my house—"

Friends who had preceded them as immigrants met them and brought them to Riverside Drive, where they found a room in a cheap rooming house, with bathroom and kitchen facilities shared by the whole floor. Their room had a breathtaking view of the Hudson River and of the New Jersey Palisades. The neon light across the water proclaimed Spry for Cooking, Spry for Baking, day and night. Later, in winter, the panoramic view had its drawbacks: the wind blew mercilessly through the many cracks in the strange American window frames, even though they tried to stop the cold air by stuffing towels and socks into the cracks.

Most of their neighbors were recent arrivals in the United States, people on their way from somewhere to somewhere else. Only the aging couple in the next room seemed to be long-term residents, an older generation of exiles, refugees who were no longer moving on. They fought bitterly, viciously, whenever they were at home. Ugly insults, uttered with atrocious German accents, filtered through the thin walls to where Paul and Helene sat amazed, listening against their will. "Why do they always fight in English," Helene whispered, "when they don't know how to speak it?"

"They must have forgotten their German," Paul whispered back. "They must be very lost here."

"It must be terrible for them," Helene said.

"Yes. We will never be like that," Paul said.

On the day after their arrival they began looking for work. They had not saved any money in Europe, nobody was saving money in Europe, and now they were faced with the necessity of paying for rent and for food. The money that the International Refugee Organization had lent them lasted only a week. Paul soon found a job as an elevator operator in one of the elegant gentlemen's clubs. Helene, who at night continued her weekly program for the Munich radio station, worked for a while as a cleaning woman, and later as saleslady in a department store on Fifth Avenue.

During their first weeks in the United States they saw each other only on weekends, for Helene left their room at nine o'clock and Paul, who worked the night shift, would leave before she came home at night. They pinned little notes for each other to their pillows. Paul usually drew a cartoon of himself in his gold-buttoned uniform, signing "Your loving and lovable lift boy." Their jobs amused them. They were in the land of unlimited opportunities; this was how one was supposed to begin. Even Christmas Eve Paul had to spend running the elevator. When he came home after midnight, Helene had prepared Christmas cookies and a present for him beneath a solitary branch of greenery.

They were surprised to find that aliens only had to register by mailing a postcard to Washington, once a year in January. They remembered the long lines at the Office for Foreigners in Munich, where they had to report, in person, every month. They recalled the scornful and belligerent attitudes of the officials, and were happy to have escaped them. They were young, they were strong, and as soon as they had saved enough, Paul would begin his studies at Columbia University.

By February they had enough money saved, and the spring term began. Paul took off his gold-buttoned uniform and went to class. He came home full of enthusiasm, happy to be in a university again.

Helene also had found a new and better-paying

occupation through the *New York Times:* she began working for a large insurance company near City Hall. Once one of Paul's fellow students asked her about her own plans. Wasn't she thinking of going back to school? She was surprised at the thought. Paul, smiling, answered for her. His own two doctorates, he said, would be sufficient for one family.

She did not give much thought to her own unlimited opportunities. After work she usually typed Paul's papers. Saturdays she spent at the public library on Forty-second Street, making notes for her radio programs and dreaming about writing a book herself one day. It would have to be a book for children and about children, that much she knew. But for the moment they needed all the money she could earn. In his second semester Paul was awarded a fellowship, but it was barely enough to cover the rent payments.

Helene's friend Anne had married a Canadian colleague, an engineering student at the university, and had left Munich shortly after they did. She wrote from Montreal, her husband's home, about continuing her studies at McGill University, about teaching a section on Chaucer to Canadian students. "Imagine your silly old Anne doing that!" she wrote.

That summer, Helene received a small inheritance. She was informed by the English lawyer that her mother had deposited the money in a London bank in her name, just before the war. It had taken him eight years, since war's end, to track Helene down across borders and continents. She was moved by the link across time and distance, by her mother's foreboding. Paul was impressed by the London bank's perseverance.

They went hunting for a better place to live and found a tiny apartment in Brooklyn Heights, in a brownstone walk-up. They could see the East River from the living room window, as it flowed into New York Bay. But here the Manhattan skyline would protect them from winter winds coming from the west. They bought a blue couch and unfinished furniture at Gimbel's, and spent many hours painting and polishing. The apartment, the first apartment that really belonged to them both, turned out to be cheerful and comfortable.

"Helene has the magic touch," their friends exclaimed. "She should go to school and become an interior decorator at Bloomingdale's!"

But Helene did not want to think about going to school. Paul had said that one family member with degrees would be enough and, besides, she liked her job in the insurance company. In the mornings she could walk to her office over the Brooklyn Bridge, facing the Manhattan skyline, watching it come near. She liked to dress the New York career-girl way, in slim dark cotton dresses with cinched waists, with pop-it chokers and white cotton gloves. She enjoyed meeting Paul in Greenwich Village after work, browsing in galleries and bookstores, discovering new restaurants, small out-of-the-way theaters. She knew that she had gained confidence in New York, liked the pace, felt part of it, in the center of things. She laughed when men stared at her and when Paul became annoyed about it. She liked her life, did not want any changes.

With the remainder of her inheritance they bought a small Morris Minor (they did not care for the toothy, finned American cars), and began to make excursions to the beaches on weekends. Rocking in the tall green waves of Gilgo Beach, arranging evening picnics on the cooling sand, driving back toward the glowing city, which never went to sleep, all that seemed unforgettable.

But one day she had not typed one of Paul's papers to his satisfaction, and Paul had one of his fits of rage, which did not seem to stop. Instead of running away from his voice as she had always done, Helene picked up the typed pages and tore them up. "If you don't like it," she said, "you can do it yourself."

Then she left the apartment to wander around the Brooklyn Heights Promenade. She was ashamed at her undignified behavior, ashamed at Paul's voice, and standing at the railing, she wept. Paul, full of remorse and apologies, found her there late at night. He reached out for her and they kissed, and across the water the lights of the Manhattan skyline blinked and glowed through the mist.

———

*T*HE NIGHTS, that autumn of Paul's departure, the nights that Helene had expected to be full of anguish were not that way at all. She realized that Paul's presence had often weighed heavily on her. At first she refused to admit to her relief, telling herself that it was only the charm of sudden solitude, the charm of being able to go down to the kitchen and make a cup of tea, in the middle of the night, the luxury of putting on a record, baking a cake, reading a book, in the middle of the night. She had always been a heavy sleeper, rarely moving, Paul always on her subconscious mind, Paul who worked so hard and must never be disturbed. Sometimes, in recent months, she had felt as if she didn't want anything more in her life than to be alone for a while: she was exhausted by constant demands, Elizabeth, Margaret, Paul; Paul, Margaret, Elizabeth.

But she found that she continued enjoying the nighttime hours, while Margaret breathed peacefully in her room, with Agatha the basset hound keeping her appreciative company. Outside, the wind blew the first drying leaves into the northernmost corner of the garden. The streetlight in front of the white house swung in the wind: on the living room wall its shadow moved back and forth.

Leaning against the white couch Helene sat, sipping her tea, remembering. As far back as she could remember, there had been Paul's anger, often barely contained, more often erupting into tantrums. At first it was directed against Paul's father, who yelled back, furiously, at once. Never before had Helene heard such explosions. Their vehemence surprised and frightened her. Later, when Paul's father had remained behind in

Prague and Paul and she were alone and dependent on each other, Paul's anger began to focus on Helene. In the beginning she had protested and tried to fight back, but she had never really learned how to fight. Afterward she was always ashamed of herself. Once, in Munich, she had locked herself in the bathroom to escape his voice, and had refused to come out even after he had long stopped, even when he had begged, for hours. Paul had to get the janitor to open the door from the outside, and then they had to pretend that it had been an accident, that the lock had jammed. When the janitor had left, shaking his head, they had fallen into each other's arms and had laughed. That was in Munich, a long time ago.

The streetlight made a scratching sound as it swung back and forth.

Several times, later, she had left the house, had set up conditions for her return: count to ten before you raise your voice, count to twenty, please count to a hundred, think of me.

Paul would laugh after he had calmed down. "I can't control myself, you know that." He would throw his head back, a gesture that had always disarmed her.

Then after the children were born, she had begged, entreated. She wanted the girls to grow up free from worry about sudden anger, she didn't want them frightened the way she herself had been. In all those years, Helene realized now, in all those years I haven't been able to convince him that his shouting was paralyzing me. I had suggested words to him, magic formulas intended to alert him, to make him think of other things, to deflect that anger. I had recited them to him like a schoolchild afraid of the dark. But nothing could stop him, the anger, when it broke, was like a flood. And I had grown to dislike the voice that permitted this flood to come and engulf me.

A branch had covered the streetlight in front of the white house, only the scratching sound remained. Every time the light appeared on the living room wall, there was also the shadow of the shivering leaves.

———

*I*N HIS THIRD SEMESTER at Columbia, Paul was appointed Teaching Instructor. The honor did not make him entirely happy, for he found the trip from Brooklyn Heights to the university much too tedious. He was exhausted before he even got there, the subway was much too noisy, it gave him headaches. The buses took much too long. New York was too hectic, the distances not fit for human life. In the spring he told Helene that he had fallen in love with Nell, a fellow student.

Nell was married, she had a husband, she had a child, and was expecting another. She was a brilliant scholar, Paul said, even the chairman was lying at her feet. Her husband did not appreciate her at all. He thwarted her intellectual growth by making her pregnant again—

"And where do I figure in this?" Helene asked.

"You have to be patient," Paul told her. "This is just an intellectual affinity. It will pass."

After the term ended in June, Paul spent almost every weekday with Nell, using the Morris Minor to go to Gilgo Beach. There would be sand between the seat upholstery, and once a pair of earrings. Helene, who had no more vacation, worked through the summer. On Sundays, when Paul was at the library, she went to Gilgo Beach alone. The tall green waves now seemed menacing, the white foam breaking over her, pulling her down, tearing at her from all sides. Driving back toward the Manhattan skyline at night was no longer romantic. It felt like driving back into a furnace, which would swallow her for another week.

Paul had received a fellowship to continue his studies in Cambridge, Massachusetts. It would be a great honor to be allowed to work in the vaults of the library there, and he was pleased about it. "That will be a good time to end the affair," he said to Helene one day. "I think I've had enough of it now."

"When will you go?" Helene asked.

"When will I go? You mean when will we go, don't you?"

"No," Helene said. "I don't mean that. I am not coming with you this time."

"What do you mean?"

"I am going to stay in New York," Helene said. "It will be good for us both to live apart. Then you can think about what you really want."

"But I have just told you what I want!" Paul raised his voice. "I have just told you that I've had enough of Nell! That's the end of this affair."

"That you've had enough of her," Helene said. "That isn't good enough for me, not anymore."

In September Helene moved to a small attic apartment around the corner. It had just become vacant. If she leaned far enough out of her only window, she could still see the Manhattan skyline. She began to take evening classes at New York University. Suddenly, the idea of going to school again did not seem at all impossible.

Paul moved to Cambridge. He came to Brooklyn Heights every weekend, bringing his books with him, writing his papers while Helene worked on hers. This way of life was too complicated, he said, all he wanted was for Helene to move to Cambridge, too, to be with him. Helene hesitated. She was enjoying her classes, enjoying New York on her own. The galleries and bookstores and theaters appealed to her, even without Paul's company. Her attic apartment was a refuge that winter, fitting around her, cozy and warm.

But in the spring Paul became ill. He was taken to the hospital with infectious arthritis. His joints were swollen and he was in great pain. For days he was unable to walk, to write, to move. "He is malnourished and overworked," the doctor said, after Helene had rushed to Cambridge. He looked at her with reproach. "You are his wife? Why do you make him live alone? Why don't you take better care of your husband?"

When they released Paul from the hospital, Helene gave up her classes and her life of independence and began to spend most of her free time driving on the Merritt Parkway and on U.S. 1, between Cambridge and New York and back again. On the radio, Frankie Laine would sing, "Nevertheless I'm in love with you." Nevertheless, Helene thought. I'm still in love with Paul. Nevertheless.

On weekends she cooked Paul's meals, made sure that he had enough to eat throughout the week, and saw to it that he did not overextend himself again. With motherly concern she watched that he took his regular doses of aspirin. In the summer she gave up her attic apartment in Brooklyn Heights. She applied for a job at the altar of the library, and moved to Cambridge. She will spend the next thirty years living in Cambridge.

—

*T*HERE IS A PAINTING, in our dining room, of Bernard's grandmother. The frame is very heavy gilt, and the woman in the painting is young, a girl. She has a sweet round face and a determined chin, and her eyes are large and dark, with a wistfulness that somehow betrays the gently smiling lips. Those eyes seem to want to curb the gleam of the young flesh under the black lace covering her décolletage; this is my acquiescing to fashion, they say, this is not the real me.

She was eighteen when the portrait was painted, Bernard tells me, and she lived until she was ninety-eight. Her husband left her after she bore him four sons, to become a Christian Scientist. To escape the family's wrath, he moved from Philadelphia to Munich, where World War I caught him, living with his Bavarian mistress. The influenza epidemic killed him, for he staunchly refused medical attention, and for many years the family in Philadelphia and the mistress in Munich haggled over who should have his body. Finally, when Hitler came to power, the Bavarian mistress was wise enough to realize that the body of a Jew, even though he was a Christian Scientist, would be better off in America.

Bernard's grandmother brought up her four sons, who were all afraid of her, without ever speaking her husband's name. When she was very old and living in an apartment at the Bellevue Stratford, she would summon her sons and their families once a week, to have Sunday dinner. From her many grandchildren she seems to have favored Bernard, the sickly boy with the many allergies, who could not see in the dark. Before dinner on Sunday afternoons, she would take him for taxi rides through Fairmount Park.

———

*T*HE MAN WHO MOVED their things from Brooklyn Heights to Cambridge in his truck was a friend of a friend's neighbor. He had been cheerful enough and full of goodwill when he departed from Brooklyn. When he finally arrived, after two whole days' travel on U.S. 1, he was extremely irritated. He had never in his life strayed so far from Brooklyn, the distance made him nervous, he said. He had no idea when he set out where Massachusetts was. He unloaded their furniture in the street. "Move it inside yourselves. I've had it," he told them.

They did just that, happy with their pastoral residence. They had rented a tiny house with a beautiful old garden not too far from campus. Their landlady had kept one of the rooms on the second floor for herself, but she would be spending the winter in Florida, she said, and would not be around much. They looked forward to being alone together in the little house: they were pleased to be living together again. But the old lady, it turned out, postponed her departure from week to week. In February she was still rustling around in her room and had stopped talking about Florida winters. So they reconciled themselves to the fact that she must have liked their company, that she was a lonely soul who rented her house in order to have contact with the outside world.

They were content. Paul was almost through with his studies, his dissertation would be ready, researched and written and corrected and bound, in time for the May deadline. And the university, not wanting to lose him, had already offered him a teaching position for the following year.

Helene was earning a good salary, and she enjoyed living in the academic community, which was so different from anything she had known before. The closeness of the graduate students' wives delighted her, and she happily joined in. She became especially fond of Olga, because they were exactly the same age and of similar backgrounds. But Olga, at twenty-six, had her hands full. She and Joseph had three little boys who were rambunctious and noisy, often overwhelming Olga, who was gentle and immersed in nineteenth-century literature. Helene was often surprised at Joseph's patience in handling his sons. She admired the sure manner with which he often took over noisy domestic situations. She had never seen a man in that role before.

In spring their garden became a pleasure for both Paul and Helene: they dug a bed and planted radishes and lettuce that would eventually result in an abundant harvest. When Paul received his American doctorate, they gave a garden party, surrounded by the things they had grown. Only the wine and the sausages had to be bought.

That afternoon their friends, graduate students and their wives, bestowed a degree on Helene: it was referred to as a Ph.T., and stood for Pulled Husband

Through. All working wives who had supplemented their husbands' fellowships were eligible, their friends said, this was the custom. Helene was very proud to have contributed to Paul's success.

During the month of Helene's summer vacation they set out in the Morris Minor, to see New England. For days they followed the small meandering roads, enchanted by the towns with Old Testament names in the hills, by the church steeples pointing to the sky like graceful chalk wands. The fishing villages in the inlets of southern Maine moved them. The tranquility of Vermont, the long ridges of the New Hampshire hills reminded Helene of her childhood in the hills of Moravia. There, too, the hills had lain folded endlessly one over the other, every ridge covered in its very own shade of blue.

All of a sudden, after the feverishness and tensions of New York, America seemed to show them its different, peaceful side. They enjoyed walking in unfamiliar surroundings, browsing in out-of-the-way country shops. They made their very first antique purchase, a small ship's lantern, from a bearded, friendly lobsterman.

After their return, before the beginning of the fall semester, they moved into a small apartment. They knew that they would miss the old garden and their vegetable beds, but not the old lady's constant presence. They bought a dining room table, and built bookshelves from pine boards and bricks, student fashion. The New England autumn glowed red and yellow outside their windows, making curtains unnecessary for the time being.

Helene deliberated for a long time before she decided that she would go to school, too. She was attracted to university life and sensed that viewing it only through her library job and through Paul's eyes might no longer be enough. Paul was not at all enthusiastic at the thought that she would not be around in the evenings. He had grown to dislike intellectual women, he said. Weren't his two doctorates enough? But she persuaded him to let her register for two evening classes in the English department of a local college. An oral report on the Metropolitan Museum's *Mlle. Charlotte du Val d'Ognes* marked her first public appearance as a student. She received an honors grade.

That fall Paul began to talk about having a child. He was thirty-four, he pointed out, he wanted to have a continuation of himself, of both of them, a little bit of immortality. For Christmas he bought Helene a nicely framed lithograph of Käthe Kollwitz's *Mother and Child*.

Helene smiled. Of course she, too, wanted children one day. But she had misgivings. There was the ever-present shadow of the bomb: one didn't know what the Cold War would bring. And, she still felt that she and Paul were not selfless enough yet to take on parental roles. On the other hand, perhaps Paul was right, perhaps it was time for them to become adults. She was used to assuming Paul's ideas, carrying out his wishes. The more she dwelled on the thought, the more she began to like the idea of a little girl with Paul's features. They were both sure that their child would be a girl.

When she became pregnant, she quit school. In the summer she quit working. It would have taken, in those days, an exceptional woman to prefer an office to the security of a nursery. Helene was not exceptional. The final month of her pregnancy was the first time in twelve years that she did not go to work as part of her daily routine. Paul's position in the department was secure, she would never have to work again, would be able to give their daughter her full attention. She enjoyed her new freedom and looked forward to her entirely new life. Motherhood was a snug harbor, in those days.

For her birthday that summer, Paul gave her Chagall's lithograph of *Mother and Child*. They had to curtail their household money for a month in order to pay for it, and they hung it in their bedroom. The baby, born in September, really was a girl, and they named her Elizabeth. They were a family.

The first two weeks of their new parenthood passed in a haze of exhaustion and Elizabeth's angry wailing. The baby, peaceful and angelic during daytime, at night was only content while being rocked or carried. They took turns rocking and carrying, wondering what Doctor Spock would say, wondering whether they were really ready for this. But in the third week of her life Elizabeth changed her habits and limited exercising her lungs only to the times that preceded her feedings. Their more experienced friends smiled patiently, for both Paul and Helene were convinced that their unusually intelligent daughter gave up because she knew that they had work to do. During that winter they worked on a commis-

sioned translation: they were transcribing and translating into English the German letters of Hilda Doolittle, a
poet born in Bethlehem, Pennsylvania. With the payment, and with their brand-new American passports,
they planned going to Europe next summer. Europe,
which they thought had been lost forever, had become
accessible and near. Student charter flights were being
organized at many universities, far less expensive than
travel by ocean liner.

They spent an idyllic summer in a small Tyrolean
village, under a gleaming glacier. They made friends
with the innkeeper and his family, and went for walks on
the willow-shaded path next to the mountain stream.
Even on hot days the stream would bring the glacier's
cold breath to the whole valley. Paul carried Elizabeth on
his shoulders high up to the fragrant mountain meadows.
The baby squealed with joy, holding onto her father's
hair, and drooled on the pretty embroidered dresses
Helene had made for her. Evenings, they sat enthralled
on the hard benches of the village barn, watching old
movies, which invariably would tear at the most sus-
penseful moments.

Only when Paul's father came from Prague for a
visit, eager to see his granddaughter, did a shadow fall
on the idyll. The relationship between father and son was
strained. Paul, Helene knew, had never forgiven his
father his extravagances, the many mistresses, and the
divorce. He blamed his father for his own sad adoles-
cence.

Helene's attempts to mediate between father and

son did not succeed. The dislike went deep, the resentments could not be bridged. Mealtimes were full of silences, broken only by Elizabeth's cooing.

———

ＡMONG BERNARD'S POSSESSIONS that were moved from Philadelphia to Cambridge was a sealed carton, which turned out to contain family photographs, the framed kind, taken by photographers. At some time they must have graced a mantel, or a side table, in the house of his parents or in the house that he and his first wife shared for twenty-four years. There is Bernard, at three, and his older brother, both in white pullovers and leggings. Bernard, at ten, with his first tie. Bernard with his mother, looking as if he had been forcefully restrained and made to lean lightly against the fragile chair she is sitting on, just for the second it took to take the photograph. Bernard's mother, reclining, with her husband looking at her adoringly, in profile. Bernard in cap and gown, the proud graduate. And, the four of them, his mother tall and elegant in a black-and-white dress and a small hat, his father and brother in white linen, Bernard himself a bit cocky and without a jacket, under palm trees.

The caption on this photograph says *Palm Beach, Spring 1946*, and that, even thirty-five years later, made me reel: in the spring of 1946 white linen and silk under palm trees were for us Europeans, still suffering from malnutrition and nightmares, strictly Hollywood, the dream factory. I hadn't known that, at that point in time, real people existed who looked like Bernard's family did.

In this photograph, Bernard and his mother stand close together, smiling. His father and Norbert, his brother, look the successful businessmen: vacationing, but nevertheless serious. Bernard tells me that the family was forever divided in this way. The mother favored the weaker, the father the stronger son. They were not very subtle about it, in the days before Freud and Jung, which could not have made for much brotherly fondness between the brothers. Norbert once told me that he was always exasperated about the little boy with the thick glasses whom he had to take along when he went to play with his friends. And Bernard must have bitterly envied the big brother who could see when he himself could not, and who could do no wrong in his father's eyes.

———

*T*HE IDYLLIC MOUNTAIN SUMMER, the return to the United States, in retrospect seems to have been the cutoff point, the watershed, the instant of change when the long complexity of Helene and Paul's life together started unraveling. After their return to the United States Paul's professional advancement began. The Russians had sent Sputnik into space the previous year, and America was trying to make up for the setback. Universities were lavishly funded. People who held the strings had taken notice of Paul, and began to compete with one another to get him on their faculties, making him one tempting offer after another. And, in order to keep him, the university promoted him every time an offer was in the wings. Each of these maneuvers seemed to Helene like an auction, like a horse trade: whoever offered the most was sure to get the horse in the end.

Paul, on the other hand, was stimulated by the whole thing. Whenever a new offer was in the air, he became animated and entertained. "That's how it's done," he said. "It's the system in this country, everybody is doing it. I'm just courted more than other people, because I'm better at my job than other people. And, as long as the game brings in more money—"

"It takes you away from me," Helene would say. But playing the complaining wife was not her style. Besides, she too was entertained, and proud of Paul's successes. She found his talent for selling himself fascinating.

Paul got what he wanted every time, his salary did get better and better. In five years he advanced from instructor to professor with tenure, then to departmental chairman, then to a name professorship. During that time Helene first heard the word *operator* used in connection with Paul's activities. Someone had whispered the word with a certain amount of awe, and had withdrawn, startled, when he caught sight of Helene.

She repudiated what to her seemed an accusation. Paul was a brilliant scholar, an outstanding teacher, not an operator. It certainly was not his fault that so many schools were eager to have him on their faculty—on the contrary: it was to his credit. It wasn't even ten years since he had come to the United States, a Displaced Person with an invalid European doctorate, entirely without money.

A handsome young president had been elected who spoke of vigor and hope, of new frontiers to be conquered, of the power of the word. It took a while for Helene to realize that for Paul, English had replaced the comfortable Czech-German mixture of languages they had always used in communicating. Moving easily between languages as they did, it was not always possible to stop and decide what was to be said in which. When she realized, she thought of the two people on Riverside Drive who had lost their language and fought so viciously in another. But of course, there was a difference: Helene and Paul never fought. If it was easier for him to address her and Elizabeth in English, why should she try to stop him, make him self-conscious? After all, their old language intimacy was intact when they spoke in bed. She continued using her Czech and German, with Elizabeth imitating her in a funny way, and Paul answering them both in English.

They moved to a better apartment on a better street, where sidewalks had borders of green lawn. They gave away the pine boards and the bricks that had served as their bookshelves, and ordered new shelving made to measure. A new Peugeot, white, replaced the creaking Morris Minor they had bought years ago out of Helene's inheritance. Helene had opted for a red car this time, but Paul ruled the suggestion out. He was a scholar, not a racing driver, he said.

But Paul's quick advancement meant more than financial comforts. It was the beginning of a new loneliness for Helene, a feeling more often suppressed than acknowledged. Paul had begun to work excessively. Articles had to be written, grants applied for, books reviewed, conferences attended, consultations held. Exams, tests, classes, committee meetings filled his days. The idea that he had to live up to his reputation, live up to his professional promise, became an obsession, a torment.

She took comfort in the belief that he would surely relax and slow down after he had reached the highest rung of the academic ladder. She drove him where he needed to be driven, protected him from Elizabeth's childish vigor and from her noisy games. She made no demands on his time. Her pride prevented her from bothering him with questions and problems of everyday life. This is how he is, she thought, shielding him from chaos: he is very ambitious and terribly conscientious, and it would be wrong of me, altogether wrong, to want to change him. He is trying to be different from his father, and I like him the way he is. It doesn't matter that he is a bit difficult. All brilliant people are difficult. I can surely manage.

She had begun to write. Her first book, conceived

and written in German, was published in Germany and was well received. After its publication she was invited to teach a course at the local college. She was happy, pleased about her achievement. She could now understand Paul's enthusiasm about exchanging ideas with young students, for she felt that way, too. She would have been surprised if someone had questioned her contentment. She was living a good life. If she sometimes missed the warmth and the conversations with Paul, she could always find it with her friends.

Soon she was ready to have another child. Both she and Paul had been only children and that, in her view, was a sad fate. Her need for family had always been strong, and she felt they needed to replace what had been lost. Elizabeth should be saved from the loneliness she herself had felt.

Elizabeth had grown into a bright and lively little girl. Her never-ending questions amazed and challenged Helene. "Why do butterflies flap their wings and airplanes never do?" the little girl would ask her. And, "When all the people on earth die, will the days still have names?" To have another child, Helene thought, would be complete happiness. It would complete their family.

———

*F*RAGILE CHILDREN WE WERE, Bernard and I. A whole ocean apart we were growing up, contracting the same childhood diseases, our mothers forever bending over our cribs, administering compresses, poultices, drops and ointments. No sooner were we recovered after one bout, when another one felled us. Born a hundred years ago, we both would have been casualties. It's only due to what pediatricians knew and perhaps surmised in the early thirties that we both survived and reached a robust middle age.

When Bernard was ten, he was taken by his mother to Arizona for six months, in order to recover from bouts with asthma. He was lucky: he got boots and chaps and a ten-gallon hat and his own horse, and could ride with the cowboys. But he was also befriended by an old gentleman, a guest in the hotel, who taught him to play chess and how to read maps. The maps, which the old gentleman studied whenever he wasn't playing chess, were military maps of World War I battlefields. The old gentleman's name was General Pershing.

When I was five, I was sent to the Tatra Mountains to recover from an especially vicious and prolonged bout with whooping cough. In the mountain hotel where I and my mother spent the two months decreed for my recovery, there were no amusements for children. I remember days that stretched, endlessly, remember lying in a striped deck chair on a balcony. An old lady lying next to me taught me to add up to a hundred, to subtract back again. And I remember wondering, If the nice and very old lady who is teaching me all this, if she dies, what will happen to all those numbers? Will they still be there?

———

MARGARET WAS BORN THE FOLLOWING FALL. When Helene's contractions began, Paul was in an important meeting and could not get away. Olga was available, and she drove Helene to the hospital. Helene did not mind; she knew about Paul's schedule. She did not mind his leaving for London the day after Margaret was born, either: he was committed to give a series of lectures in England. Having babies, after all, was a woman's business. Paul called it division of labor, and of course he was right.

Relief came from other women. Catherine, whose baby was due the following month, brought Helene and the newborn home from the hospital. Olga brought over warm dinners every night. Sophie saw to it that Elizabeth was picked up in the morning, taken to school, and brought home again in the afternoon. Ruth did Helene's marketing, Pat took care of the laundry. It was an expression of female solidarity a long time before the women's movement. Chores got done cheerfully and without fuss. Helene was almost glad of Paul's absence. She found it much easier to ask help from other women.

Paul was still being wooed by one university or another, by one institute or another, and his university heaped honors upon him. And, as months went by, as one season followed another, one semester followed another, Helene began to see that her hope, that Paul would lighten his work load after he had proven himself, that a plateau could be reached where he could exist without feeling harassed and pressed for time, had been in vain. More meetings were added to his schedule, more official functions, more trips to universities in America and abroad.

She felt sorry for him when she looked at his appointment calendar. Men really don't have it easy, she thought, for it seemed to her that there was barely time left for him to teach his students. But watching Paul, she saw that he was thriving, full of energy, full of ideas, enjoying and savoring his success. By supporting him, she thought, I must be providing the sustenance he needs, and by supporting him, I am creating the family I need. This is the division of labor he speaks about. Even some years later, when the girls were growing up and time had confused memories of those years and overlaid them with later knowledge, Helene would re-member that this was the kind of life Paul wanted.

After a while it no longer occurred to her that she could wish for things to be different. Paul was well, the girls were healthy. Elizabeth, in elementary school, was sturdy and mischievous, with big blue eyes and dark Paul-hair, and a quick intelligence. Margaret was a friendly, red-cheeked baby bundle, who spent the sunny part of the day on the porch, kicking her feet like a rider, rocking her baby carriage. Helene's teaching hours and housekeeping did not leave her much free time. But on some occasions she managed to relax, exchanging housewifely humor and babysitting with her friends, all of whom were rearing children. Thus she gained a wry perspective on her life, and an occasional free afternoon. She used these afternoons to write her second book, a memoir of growing up in Central Europe before and during the war, about her family, which no longer existed. She would discuss what she was writing with Paul, ask for his advice, and he gave it willingly.

As Elizabeth became older and acquired friends, and as Margaret turned into a toddler and began talking a blue streak, it was easier to speak only English with the children. Paul had been doing that for a long time, anyway: it was too difficult for him to switch languages and cultures once he got home, he explained. Helene would answer and address him in Czech or in German, and she felt comfortable with this arrangement. At night, when they were close and alone, they would still use their own familiar mixture of languages. Often their linguistic predicament made them laugh.

Whenever Paul went into one of his shouting fits, she remained quiet, in order not to frighten the children even more. Sometimes, standing back and listening to

Paul's angry accented English, she would be reminded of their neighbors on Riverside Drive. But the worry was no more than a fleeting shadow, a slight ripple on the river of their existence.

Her own anger was aroused only once during those early family years: the day Paul had one of his large staff call to tell her to make sure to have the house clean, because he was bringing home unexpected guests. She was not at all disturbed by his lack of trust in her housekeeping. The fact that he had not found the time to tell her himself mattered more to her, rankled. On that day she stopped in her tracks and thought of making a dramatic gesture, of leaving. On that day she confronted him. But Paul seemed to face her anger without any trace of comprehension. "I just don't understand what you are so mad about," he said, shaking his head. "Can't you see how busy I am? Look what a good life you have!"

The "look what a good life you have" became, after some time, a recurrent refrain. It was said every time Helene started to talk about the distance that she began to sense between them, about Paul's edginess and impatience. She did not raise the point often, because she invariably felt foolish afterward. Why complicate things, she would tell herself. Paul was so much more brilliant than other men. How could she compare him with others, how could she want to apply ordinary standards? As a matter of fact, weren't they both rather talented and unusual? Weren't they both successes, living proof of what the American dream was about? Why complicate things with too many questions?

ELIZABETH CAME HOME for the long Thanksgiving weekend, that fall after Paul's departure. Helene picked her up at the train station, her nineteen-year-old daughter, who looked almost exactly the way she herself used to look, except for the flamboyant dark hair, Paul's hair. They talked past each other cautiously; they always needed a while to get used to one another, to get used to the fact that they were very close.

Saying good night to her mother, after the first evening, Elizabeth became upset. "You don't talk to each other at all, you and Daddy," she said, on the verge of tears. "You are a pair of stubborn East Europeans! I just don't understand you! You have to go for counseling; Sue's parents went, and it helped them! They didn't get divorced! And they fought terribly and there was a woman—Sue told me all about it! I will go see Daddy tomorrow and I'm going to tell him that I insist, that you both have to do it! I will blackmail him if he doesn't want to, I will tell him that I will fail math if you both don't go!" Elizabeth threw herself on her bed, sobbing.

Helene bent down and kissed Elizabeth's shoulder, stroked her head. She promised to obey, to find a marriage counselor right away, on Monday. Elizabeth turned over, patted her hand, calmed down. The following day she came home from town, beaming. Daddy said yes, she reported, Daddy will go for marriage counseling. It's up to Helene to find someone to go to.

Mrs. Nangle's office was next to a shabby police station, in a building with walls made entirely of glass, the Mental Health Center. It did look slightly surreal to Helene: mental health, made of glass, right next to the almost invisible police. She quickly glanced at Paul, whom she hadn't seen for two months. If we were not estranged, she thought, we would wink at each other now. But Paul did not meet her eyes. Where is his sense of humor, Helene wondered. We always understood each other without too many words. Wasn't it this special wordless communication for which I loved him most?

Paul helped Helene with her coat, and Helene realized that Mrs. Nangle took note of the action. Helene was tempted to pat Mrs. Nangle's shoulder, to tell her that what she was seeing was merely a superficial gesture, a form of civility that was part of Paul, that had nothing to do with feelings. It occurred to her that this friendly woman would do no more than simplify and touch the surfaces. Panic enfolded Helene. Choosing Mrs. Nangle was a mistake. They should never have let a woman counsel them, certainly not a woman of Mrs. Nangle's kind, well-meaning, and probably without a doctorate. Paul will not take her seriously, Helene thought, he will not consider her his equal.

Outside, a December rain was beating against the large windowpane. Many rivulets of water ran down the wall of glass. Helene leaned back in her chair.

"Why did you come here?" Mrs. Nangle asked.

Helene looked at Paul. Paul shrugged. I wish I knew, was what his shrug implied. In one of our family albums, Helene remembered, we have a snapshot taken at our wedding, we were sitting just like this, on two chairs set side by side, facing a desk. But I was holding a bouquet, and Paul was winking at me. Then.

"We are," Helene began haltingly, seeing that Paul would not answer, "we are in a crisis. We have reached a crisis in our lives." She began describing what happened that September Sunday, told about her repressed anger of the previous summer, about the years of Paul's silences. She took great pains not to leave anything out. Several times she felt Paul looking at her. He is surprised, she thought, that I am talking so much. When he was around, with other people, I always left the talking up to him. "Perhaps," she continued, "perhaps we can find each other through this crisis? Maybe we can learn again how to talk to each other?" She became aware that she had folded her hands as she spoke, in a supplicatory gesture, and she quickly put her hands behind her back, embarrassed. "Margaret," she said, "Margaret is so young, she is just twelve. I have a student in my class, her parents were divorced when she was twelve, and she is still so sad, so lost—" She stopped herself, fearing that her voice would break. Paul would not like that. Paul never liked to see her with her nose red.

When Helene had fallen silent, Mrs. Nangle looked at Paul. "And what do you have to say?"

Paul was smiling now. "It is much too late," he said.

"Much too late for reconciliations and such. I want to be divorced, and I will be divorced. Irretrievable breakup, as the lawyers say."

Mrs. Nangle seemed surprised. She said, "Why did you come here when you are so certain?"

Paul stopped smiling. He shrugged. I wish I knew, his shrug said.

"Would you like to tell why you are so certain?" Mrs. Nangle prodded.

Paul sighed. "I've been unhappy, deeply unhappy for years," he said. "My wife had an affair—"

"Did she?" Mrs. Nangle interrupted. "When was that?"

"I don't remember," Paul shrugged. "Some time ago."

"Twelve years ago," Helene said quietly. "It was twelve years ago." An affair. Gerd.

"And you've been deeply unhappy since then?" Mrs. Nangle asked.

"Exactly," Paul said.

"Did you ever talk to your wife about it, in those twelve years?" Mrs. Nangle asked.

"I was too busy. I am a very busy man," Paul said.

"Why didn't you ever tell me?" Helene said. Her hands, which she was pressing together behind her back, were damp and sticky. "Why now, after twelve years?"

Paul threw his head back. He laughed as if Helene had just told him a joke. How I have always loved this gesture, Helene thought. She said quietly, "I told Gerd at the time, twelve years ago, that I would not see him anymore. That I would not leave you and the children. He came to Geneva that time, and I told him. Because of you and the children. And I told you, twelve years ago, that it was over. You cannot start blaming me now, after all this time—"

"And why can't I?" Paul said. "Why can't I, if I feel like it?"

Helene shook her head. I cannot follow his thoughts, she realized. What does he mean? Affairs were never supposed to mean much, his certainly didn't—And then she suddenly knew. Paul is lying. He is justifying himself, he has invented this to justify the divorce to himself. He will depict me as the cheating wife now, to himself. Once more the memory of Paul on the hallway floor, last summer, after he fell down the stairs. In falling, he ripped pictures off the wall, there was blood on the back of his head—She realized that Paul had been talking for a while. She straightened, listened.

"—and I could never develop, never write the big book I wanted to write, I was so deeply unhappy," Paul was saying.

"And you never ever mentioned this, in twelve years?" Mrs. Nangle asked. "That is surprising."

Paul shrugged.

"Let me ask you something else," said Mrs. Nangle. "Did you love Helene, before you decided to get a divorce?"

Paul thought for a while, his finger at his temple. "I don't think I ever loved Helene," he said.

"But you still stayed married to her for thirty years?" Mrs. Nangle asked.

Paul laughed. "The marriage was purely a matter of convenience," he said.

"Hmmph," said Mrs. Nangle. "A thirty-year convenience."

"You are lying, Paul," Helene said. "We have never lied to each other, but you are lying now. There is no point in talking further." She turned to Mrs. Nangle. "It does not make any sense to talk further, none at all. This man is lying." Abruptly, she got up, feeling that she would suffocate if she stayed a minute longer. It didn't matter any longer what Paul thought. He was lying.

Mrs. Nangle held Helene's hand for a moment. "Feel free to come again," she said. "Later perhaps."

Outside it was raining hard. Water coursed down the walls of the Mental Health Center, down the steps of the police station, a real New England downpour. Helene ran to the car ahead of Paul, jumping over little rivers of rain. She slammed the car door and started driving off before Paul could get in. She was surprised, almost shaken, when in the rearview mirror she discovered that Paul had expected, even now, even after what had been said, to be driven to town, to his class, as always.

———

*I*N THE SUMMERS, it was much cheaper to sublet their apartment and go to Europe again than to stay home. But the small Tyrolean village where they had spent their first idyllic European vacation no longer suited Paul. It was much too rustic, much too rough and primitive. He needed city air, not the smell of dung. Helene, her activities limited by Elizabeth's small-child needs, then spent many summer days in French and Austrian furnished city apartments. Paul would leave in the morning and go to the library, returning for supper at six o'clock, maintaining his winter schedule. After Margaret was added to the family, it was much less expensive and more practical for Helene to stay in the Tyrolean village with the children while Paul traveled restlessly from one capital to another, checking up on his European colleagues' publications. Whenever Helene could arrange it, they met on weekends, in different cities. On such weekends, their American daily life very far away, they felt suspended in time and place. They could pretend that they had just met, that they had no life together except the present moment, that they might never meet again. On these weekends, they would again speak their comfortable mixture of languages, their secret code.

But Helene could not get away often enough. Neither of them had any family who could have assumed care of the children from time to time, even briefly. Every hour that Helene did not spend with the children had to be organized, arranged, and paid for. She agreed, she even suggested, that Paul should travel by himself when he needed rest and when she herself was not free. If she had to be tied down by the children, at least he should not feel fenced in. From these trips, Paul would return cheerful and laden with presents, beautiful things for the three of them. "Daddy is our summer Santa!" the girls would frolic.

After one of Paul's vacation trips Helene discovered among his papers several photographs of an unknown young woman. When letters began arriving, she thought fleetingly that she should make a scene, threaten to leave. But she would not have known where to go: she had no substantial amount of money on her own. Besides, she and Paul by then were connected, connected by almost twenty years of friendship and affinity. It would take more than a summer adventure to destroy what they shared.

When the letters were followed by a list of requests, she sent the desired items. Paul barely read the letters when they arrived, left them lying around. Helene felt sorry for the unknown young woman. And, for a flash of a second, very deep and only unwillingly acknowledged, she also felt a tiny spark of pleasure at the thought that Paul still found the time to be interested in women. It seemed to give him the human dimension that was in danger of becoming lost, the human dimension that she was beginning to miss in him. It is not too late, she thought, we will find each other again.

———

*B*ERNARD AND HIS FIRST WIFE married fresh out of college, as was the custom in the early fifties. The wedding took place at the country club, and there is a photograph among the photographs in the carton, of young Bernard, very proper in tuxedo and very wide pants, very enthusiastically hugging a pretty smiling girl. They left right after the reception, by limousine for Idlewild Airport (where we had arrived the previous fall, by refugee plane), then by a twin-engine Cessna for Hamilton, Bermuda. They were both almost-virgins, as was the custom in the early fifties. On their wedding night the bride refused to go to bed, instead resolutely demanding a pail and a mop from the hotel management. The tile floor of their room did not seem clean enough to her. Whether this bade well for her future life I would not presume to judge. And since Bernard, when I met him thirty years later, was slightly prejudiced on the topic, I will probably never know. At any rate, three daughters were born during the course of the next four years, which even now makes me feel a tinge of strong female solidarity with the pretty girl in the photograph:

even with live-in help, even with unlimited funds, this could not have been easy for her. Bernard sometimes tells me of putting the girls to bed, of singing them to sleep every night, after he came home from work. But I know better. Days with three toddlers, even with live-in help, must have been very long. Eventually, the pretty girl found ways to escape. She played a lot of tennis and regularly fell in love with her tennis instructors. It was a man of that particular profession who, twenty-four years later, when the Commonwealth of Pennsylvania had not yet recognized no-fault divorces, was named corespondent in the divorce proceedings. That the said corespondent ultimately went back to his own wife can no longer be part of my story.

———

LIFE'S MOST SIGNIFICANT MOMENTS very often happen at most inopportune times. When Anne's phone call came, at five o'clock one winter afternoon in 1964, Helene was just stirring the sauce for dinner. In her high chair, Margaret loudly demanded her cup of juice, and Elizabeth, in tears, was confiding about her best friend's recent lack of friendship. In their cage, the gerbils were frantically running the wheel, which Helene had forgotten to oil the week before.

"Helene," Anne said, from Montreal, "I want to tell

you straightaway. You know that I'm no good at beating around the bush—"

Helene laughed. "I know that," she said. "What's up, Annie?"

"I have spoken to Gerd," Anne said. When Helene didn't answer, she continued, quickly. "We went to Frankfurt with Andrew, just came back from there, one of his engineering conferences—"

"You have spoken to Gerd," Helene said. From very far away, the squeaking of the gerbils' wheel continued. Elizabeth, thank heavens, had stopped crying and had handed Margaret her cup.

"Yes," Anne said. "He was there, one of the participants. I recognized him right away. He didn't know me, of course—"

"You have spoken to Gerd," Helene repeated. The kitchen wall had made a turn, in time with the squeaking wheel.

"—but I told him who I was, that I knew you. You know what one says in such situations—"

"Yes," Helene said.

"—and he turned white, I have never seen anybody like that—"

"What—what did he say?" Helene whispered.

"He was just as stunned as you are now," Anne said. "I gave him your address."

"My address," Helene said.

"Yes, he asked me for it. He will write to you. And you should answer him, this time."

"I have to go," Helene whispered, in haste. "My sauce is burning up."

The sauce, at this point, was hopelessly scorched. With shaking hands, Helene removed the pan from the stove. Then her legs gave out, and she groped for a chair, sat down.

"The traitor," Elizabeth said angrily. "I will never be friends with her again!"

The gerbils had given up running and stood, their little hands clutching the bars of their cage, squealing for their dinner.

Two days later, when she had stopped her hands from shaking, Helene called Anne back. "Please tell me everything," she pleaded. "What else did he say?"

"Well, it was a noisy conference," Anne said. "You know how engineers like to talk—"

"Come on, Annie," Helene said.

Anne giggled. "All right, all right. He lives in Frankfurt, and he had a wedding ring, if that's what you are asking—"

"I'm not," Helene said.

"His hair is grey, I think—but with blond men one can't really tell. He works for a chemical engineering firm. He said he would be going to Lisbon next summer as a consultant. They are building some huge bridge there, and he is supposed to be measuring the rust potential, I don't understand the technicalities—the mention of your name hit him square between the eyes—is that what you want to hear?"

"Yes," Helene said. "That's what I want to hear."

Because, she thought after she hung up—and she wasn't even amazed at the coincidence, since she had at that very moment already accepted the inevitability of it—because we are going to Lisbon, too, next summer.

———

*I*T'S SO LONG AGO, but I still remember everything. First I was angry when you didn't answer. Later I understood why you didn't. When I came back from Louisiana, in 1947, I looked for you everywhere. I wrote to the International Red Cross. But there were so many people lost and missing in those days. And Germany was so isolated from everything. Then, in 1951, I finally got permission to go to Prague. I found your street, even learned to say it in Czech, because people refused to talk to me when I spoke German. But nobody knew you, or maybe they pretended that they didn't. I had the feeling that you are still alive, and that you are in the West somewhere. By then I was suspect in Dresden, could not go to university, the former American P.O.W. So I went over the green border, began studying in Frankfurt. I still looked for you. But I knew that I would have to give up looking, too many years had gone by. I got married. We have two boys, and they are great children. I thought I was happily married, until I heard that you were alive. What are we going to do now?

Helene, in her kitchen, folded the letter, carefully put it away. What are we going to do now? she repeated. It's so long ago, twenty-one years. I am no longer the girl you knew. But I still remember our walk over White Mountain, you carried my school bag and pretended to blow the bugle. Then you no longer wanted to play war, not even the Thirty Years' War. I still remember your hand on my shoulder when we walked around the castle built in the shape of a star, the castle named Star. And I remember the clouds as we looked up at them and gave them names. But no matter how many times I rewind the film, reel by reel, it's only memories. We cannot go back, we are both committed to others, our previous selves are no longer reachable. Or are they?

———

*P*AUL HAD RECEIVED A FELLOWSHIP to do research in Switzerland for one year. He had left earlier in June, by plane, because he had no time and patience for sea voyages, and Helene had decided to go by ship. It took a tremendous amount of luggage to transplant a family of four for one year. Paul had lectures to give in Lisbon, and they were to meet there and spend the summer before going to Geneva in the fall.

She found the slow-motion calm of shipboard life soothing, and she enjoyed the unexpected hours of solitude granted her when both girls developed a passion for the ship's nursery and the young woman in charge there. She watched for hours as the horizon bobbed up and down between the rods of the ship's railing. This is how we are, she thought, we too are bobbing up and down, up and down, no matter what we try to do. She was thirty-six, a faculty wife, her daily existence had run its course in well-worn tracks between classes, visits to the pediatrician, school assemblies, and dinner parties for members of the faculty.

Then the detachment from her everyday life began to cast its spell on her. She felt free, and very happy. She had written to Gerd that she, too, would be in Lisbon that summer, and had realized that Gerd, too, had accepted the coincidence, the inevitability of it.

That past winter, the paperback edition of her first book had come out in Germany, and she had received a substantial one-time royalty payment. She had arranged, with a Lisbon employment agency, for an English-speaking student to watch the girls in the afternoons, and on some evenings. This would allow her to exchange her role of mother for that of adultress.

———

*I*T WAS A RECORD-BREAKING WINTER for New England, that winter after Paul had left. The thermometer on the kitchen window of the white house could no longer register the cold: there were no numbers and no lines for it. The oil bills were staggering. The oil truck, it seemed to Helene, had barely turned the corner before it was back again to fill the empty tank. And Paul, who had never, in their married life, cared where his salary went, had begun to scrutinize every bill: two households were more expensive to keep than one. The pipes in his unused bathroom froze, water had to be kept running there day and night. Helene had to keep blowing at the pipes with her hair dryer, the way the plumber had taught her.

The kitchen, on the north side of the white house, was much too cold to sit and eat in. Every night now Helene made a fire in the living room fireplace, for during the summer she had ordered, and with Margaret's help had stacked, enough wood to last for three winters. Margaret had brought the kitchen table into the living room. There they had their meals, read, played chess. Margaret had pulled Helene's second book from the shelf, the one Helene had written about her family, about growing up in Central Europe, published in Germany six years ago. She began reading it for the first time, very slowly, for her German was spotty, asking for help with the long words. The following night she picked it up again, seemed engrossed, the way she used to be when she was still reading about the Bobbsey Twins. "Gee, Mom," she said, "this is good. Did you write it just for the German people?"

"I did," said Helene. "Why do you ask that?"

"Well," Margaret shrugged, uncomfortable about having to explain herself. "I mean, we are Americans. Shouldn't Americans read this, too?"

Helene looked up. "You mean—I should translate the book?"

"Sure," Margaret said. "You can do it!"

At night the long icicles hanging from every roof looked like fantastic fairyland decorations in the glow of the streetlamp. The fire in the fireplace had not died yet, the embers crackled and blinked with a reddish twinkle. Outside the windows, the crackling and blinking was icy white.

Margaret is right, Helene thought. I ought to stop feeling sad and angry, begin doing something for myself. Five or ten years from now, there will have to be something besides the sadness and the anger, when I think back on the divorce, when I think back on this year.

The kitchen table looked strangely misplaced in front of the fireplace. After she had finished Helene's book, Margaret had gone back to a chess game and had left the figures standing. Margaret was almost in the championship class: Helene had not yet won a single game against her. Sometimes she was checkmated before she could even collect her wits. My father, Helene remembered now, was an excellent chess player, much better than I. I wonder if Margaret would checkmate him, too? The poor girls. How often I had felt sorry for them because they had to grow up almost in a vacuum, with just the two of us. There were no grandparents to compete for the little girls' favors, no aunts and uncles to take over for a while. We were the typical nuclear family, the four of us. We are immigrants, Helene had always told the children, that's why we don't have a large family like all your friends. Instead, we have a solidarity with each other, we understand one another because we are dependent on one another, because that's all we have. We have no family traditions, because all our traditions were destroyed during the war. Instead, we have very traditional feelings for one another, which do not need many words or explanations. The girls, she had always thought, understood what she meant.

What will happen now, Helene wondered, now that they have seen that the solidarity and the feelings were not worth a penny? When they have witnessed that it just takes moving one's shirts, for solidarity and friendship to be forgotten? Will they forgive us for what we are doing? What kind of life did we really live for thirty years, when it took only a moment to shake it all off?

The logs in the fireplace had stopped blinking. Only the icy whiteness outside still crackled. Helene turned off the living room light and went upstairs. I will have to stop this, she told herself, holding onto the railing in the dark. I will have to stop thinking about Paul. Five or ten years from now, there will have to be something more than sadness and anger.

———

"*I* AM CONVINCED I owe you my life," Gerd said to Helene. "I know it sounds very melodramatic, but it's as simple as that. That summer of 1944, in France, you were on my mind all the time. I wrote you about that."

"I remember," Helene said.

"And then came the moment, a split second, where I had the choice, either to step on a land mine, be shot, or be taken prisoner. But I had to live to see you again, so the choice was easy—" He took her hand. "I didn't know it would take twenty-one years to see you again."

They smiled at each other, seeing in each other the young people they once were. Twenty-one years ago, the war had been all around them, even on the quiet paths of the park surrounding the castle named Star, on White Mountain near Prague. Now, the green wine in their glasses threw pale green sparkling reflections on the white tablecloth. The waiter hovered nearby, unobtrusively brushing nonexistent crumbs from spotless dinner plates. Outside, the half circle of Santo Amaro Beach was speckled with yellow umbrellas. Women sat under them, knitting. Closer to the edge of the water the spread-out blankets, each with its own radio, of the local teenagers formed another half circle. Only the Portuguese children in their round straw hats, running back and forth, interrupted the beach symmetry.

Above the sea, vertical lines of sun streamed out of the clouds. And in the distance, toward the city, the two arms of the unfinished bridge were moving closer to each other every day.

That summer, Helene was leading a strange double life. Her mornings were full of marketing, cooking, playing with the children, paying attention, being there. Afternoons and a few evenings belonged to Gerd. They met almost every day in the small restaurant in Santo Amaro, near Gerd's lab, where the waiters would keep their table for them and welcome them like friends. It seemed to Helene that never before had a summer been so beautiful, with the sun taking hours to set, until only a thin line of orange stayed long into the night, above the black Atlantic.

"We will never see it like this again," she told Gerd.

"We will always see it like this," Gerd said.

She had told Paul about Gerd. They had always been able to avoid telling lies to each other. Paul had accepted her confession with an indifference that surprised and hurt Helene: she had expected and almost hoped for his usual violent outburst.

"Just do what you have to do," Paul said. "We don't own each other. But don't tell me about it, spare me the details. I have a lot of work to do."

She spared Paul the details. That summer, she would have found it difficult to speak about the pleasure she felt when Gerd was near her. She would have found it difficult to describe the magic that the blue-and-white city had acquired for her, because of Gerd. She could not have spoken to Paul about the confusion that her double life had brought upon her, not about the moments of fierce longing, of the longing for her home in America, a longing for the safe routine of the university community, for early morning classes and afternoon teas. She could not have spoken about her half wish that she might find her peace again in the security of daily life.

When the bittersweet summer was nearing its end,

she wept. The fragrant fall on Lake Geneva, with the Dents du Midi rising beautifully above the lake mist every morning, was full of sadness. The Lisbon summer stayed in her memory with a sweet, almost imperceptible pang of regret. But as the days passed, she knew that her ties to Paul and to the children were stronger than her wish to escape, to relive her youth. It was not her way to wish for the impossible. It was not her way to long for the past. She had grown up in wartime, and was too much aware of the destruction that selfishness could cause.

When Gerd came to Geneva that winter to persuade her to leave Paul, she begged him to forget their summer, to forget her.

"It is too late for us," she told him. "Too many people would be hurt."

He argued with her. "What about us? We are not important?"

"We would be carrying the weight of their pain with us forever," she said. She looked at him, trying to memorize his face under the grey sky of Cornarvain Airport.

He did not kiss her when his flight was called. Like twenty-one years ago, he only touched her temples with the tips of his fingers, very gently. Then he turned and went away.

The year on Lake Geneva, far from the American work schedules and pressures, was beneficial for Paul. By and by his sense of humor emerged again and his urbanity, the qualities she had always liked and admired in him. When the stiffness and nervousness began to peel off him like a coat of armor, she began to rediscover the old Paul, whom she had sometimes feared lost forever.

When she and the children were on their way back to America after that year, the memory of Gerd and of the enchantment and restlessness of the past summer had faded into an opaque hue. The Lisbon Bridge, she knew, was built now, the two arms had met each other in the middle. Traffic streamed across it, endlessly, day and night. But the stream of her daily life flowed under and past it. She knew now that she belonged with Paul, who loved her in his own way. They were friends: they knew each other's weaknesses, were tuned into each other. They were each other's family, connected by their past, for richer and for poorer, for better and for worse.

She would have liked to talk to Paul, who had rushed home ahead of her, about her feelings on her return.

———

*I*N THE YEAR OF THE LORD 1620, on the fields of White Mountain near Prague, a battle was fought between hastily assembled Protestant armies and the army of Catholic Prince Buquoy of Bavaria. The battle, or its outcome, had far-reaching consequences for the small states and principalities of Central Europe: for the next thirty years, there would be no peace. The victory of the Catholics on White Mountain meant doom for the followers of Jan Hus in the lands of Bohemia and Moravia. The king fled the country by night. Protestant noblemen were publicly beheaded on Prague's Old Town Square. The town gentry either had to convert or leave. Small folk, who called themselves Brethren, scattered into the countryside like so many field mice. The reign of the Habsburgs began.

Some of the Brethren had fled north, all the way into the woods of Saxony. There, in the course of two generations, they forgot their Bohemian and Moravian tongues, made their names sound German, became Saxons. But they never forgot to call themselves Brethren, Moravian Brethren.

They were excellent artisans, pious and industrious, and impressed and fired the imagination of the nobleman on whose lands their grandfathers had been allowed to settle. This man, Count Zinzendorf, believed himself to be a leader of men, chosen to go out into the world to convert heathens to Christian beliefs. Since there were no more heathens in Europe at that time, Count Zinzendorf turned his attention to the new lands across the ocean. With a handful of Moravian followers he set out for the New World. On Christmas Eve of the year 1741, they finally arrived in the hills of Pennsylvania, which must have reminded them of the hills of Saxony and perhaps, atavistically, of the hills of Moravia. They were warmly welcomed by the Lenape Indians. And, near the confluence of the Delaware and the Lehigh Rivers, they founded the town of Bethlehem.

———

*B*UT AFTER THE GENEVA YEAR, after returning home, Helene found Paul again fully withdrawn under his professorial armor of importance. He was working obsessively, was often harassed and irritable. There barely was time to talk about daily occurrences. Feelings were put aside to gather dust and, after a while, were forgotten.

The children turned nine and three that fall. They were lively, noisy, full of spirit, and ever present, needing to be brought up, driven places, restrained, entertained and kept clean. When Paul was around, in need of his afternoon rest or working in his study, they also had to be kept quiet.

At times, after Helene had taken care of the household and had prepared her class for the next day, she sighed with exhaustion. She could not ask Paul for help. Paul didn't have the time. Besides, he was impatient and often sarcastic with the girls, was appalled at their unreasonableness, shouted instead of explaining and negotiating. The girls reacted by being especially difficult and rambunctious whenever he was around. Again, it was much simpler to ask help from friends when she felt at the end of her rope. Their help was always available: a dinner cooked and delivered, a car pool, an extra bag of groceries picked up at the supermarket, a family trip that would include her girls. Friends offered her comfort in their gardens, the simple solace of a shared cup of tea, of a frustrating event recalled with laughter.

At times, a thought would come up like an unexpected ripple in the stream, the thought that her own life was quite different from the lives of her friends. She did not want to dwell on comparisons, tried to suppress the thought when it arose. But sometimes, as women were talking more and more about being liberated, about doing their thing, the comparison would force itself on her almost against her will.

She noticed that Olga across the street went to her classes, worked on her dissertation, while Joseph took care of the laundry and drove their youngest to school. She noticed that Sophie's husband had long conversations with his children and spent much time planning and building an electric train yard with them, giving Sophie time to get away to do her thing, refinishing antiques.

Whenever Helene started dwelling on these observations, she became angry at herself. Such thinking is quite unproductive besides being unfair, she told herself. These men are Americans. They see the role of father differently. They have been trained and taught to help, to be involved, it's a leftover from pioneer days—

But she did not always succeed in excusing Paul's lack of interest. Then she would beg. "It would be so nice," she would tell Paul, "it would be so nice if you could make friends with the girls. They need you, and they will grow up so fast."

"I don't understand what you are complaining about," Paul would answer.

Helene would laugh a bit nervously, because she could see that a conversation of this kind was not to Paul's liking. "I'm not complaining at all," she would say.

"I'm always home for dinner," Paul would say, and the vein on his forehead would stand out, "I don't drink, I work hard. I'm the ideal husband, don't you see?"

"I do," Helene would laugh. "I do. I'm not complaining, far from it. But the children—"

"The children are your responsibility," Paul would raise his voice. "I simply don't have time for that kind of togetherness! I'm not your typical American husband!"

Helene would fall silent. I am being silly, she thought. What on earth gave me the idea that I should compare Paul with other men? Isn't he by far the most brilliant of them? Don't I have a good life? Why spoil it with requests that Paul is just not made to meet? If he is remiss, I can make it up to the children, be with them for both of us.

She did have a good life, and she enjoyed it. There were the long, relaxed summer days in the Tyrolean village, under the glacier, which sometimes glowed like the chalky glacier spires in German Romantic paintings. There were the girls, tanned and delighted, flitting between the cow barn and the swimming pool, setting out on important expeditions to bring blueberries from high slopes. There were the evenings, when one could see chamois climbing the rocks across the valley in the last sharp evening light. With her binoculars she could make out the paths where she and the girls had wandered on previous climbs. And there were the mornings, before the girls awoke, before the sun came up over the craggy rocks across the valley, so vibrant that one could feel them on one's lips, in one's eyes, in one's fingertips. It seemed to Helene that this was endless happiness, a good woman's life.

There were the winter afternoons at home, when the three of them squeezed into the old Peugeot with their equipment and drove to the skating rink or to the hills and ski lifts. The girls learned early how to ski and skate. Elizabeth was on the figure-skating team, and Helene spent many afternoons watching her daughter and cheering with other proud parents. On the ski slopes, the girls quickly surpassed her abilities and moved on to the advanced runs, leaving her and her careful turns down below. She liked to watch them coming down toward her, their bodies graceful, their cheeks glowing, stopping with a great stem christie two feet away from her, sending a cloud of snow all over her own skis.

Once in a while, a recurring dream upset her. The dream was of herself among a group of people, suddenly discovering that all her clothes were gone, trying to flee, naked and horrified, trying to run away before anyone found her out. She would wake from the dream, heart pounding, legs twitching from the exertion of the impossible flight. Then, after she had calmed down, she would wonder: What is it that I cannot let them find out about me? What secrets am I hiding? Why am I so afraid?

———

*E*LIZABETH HAD COME from college for Christmas recess, filling the silent white house with noise and action again. One night she sat down next to Helene on the living room couch, looking pensive. "I've thought a lot about you, Mom," she said after a while. "And do you know what I promised myself? That I will never, never spoil a man the way you've always spoiled Daddy."

Helene looked at her almost grown-up daughter, at her blue eyes and the shock of dark hair, Paul's hair, and the nineteen-year-old intensity and spirit, so reminiscent of Paul when he was young. "I'm sure you won't," she said. "I think that girls will not want to spoil their men anymore, things have changed. You are a different generation, you know." She patted Elizabeth's arm. "Girls now stand on their own two feet. No man will ever be their master. For my generation it was different—"

"I don't know why," Elizabeth said fiercely. "I really don't! Why should it have been so different for you?"

Helene thought for a while. "I guess," she said, "our destinies were in being wives, just like our mothers were, you know. We were brought up with the idea that we of course would get married, and that we of course would see our happiness in making our man's life easier.

Husbands provided shelter. And wives did the nurturing—"

"Oh, nonsense!" Elizabeth cried out, impatient. "Can't you see what nonsense that is?"

"I see it now," Helene said. "Of course I do. But when I was your age, your father and his welfare were the most important things in the world for me."

Elizabeth looked at her, frowning.

"And then," Helene continued, "after what the war did to our families, mine and Daddy's, I wanted to create a family again. And the only way I knew how, was to re-create what I had known when I was little—"

"But girls have to find their own selves," Elizabeth said. "If they don't know who they are, then all the happiness in the world means nothing! Just look at what Daddy did—he thought he could do anything, just because you were at his beck and call, you served him!"

"I was better," Helene said quietly, "much better than some women my age. I did have a teaching job, and I did write books."

"That's true," Elizabeth admitted. She patted Helene's hand. "But Mom, didn't it ever occur to you that he might—that he might leave? Because you made everything so easy for him?"

Helene considered Elizabeth's words. She was grateful for her daughter's patting gesture: she remembered herself doing the same at some important conversation, some years ago. "No," she said. "It never occurred to me."

"The way he always was, selfish—you knew that, didn't you?"

"Yes," Helene said. "I knew that. But I, you see, I always identified with him. We were always a team. It was always us against the world. We were in it together, we were allies from the very beginning. That he would turn against me one day—no, that I never imagined. It didn't occur to me."

I did tell Elizabeth the truth, Helene thought later, remembering the conversation. It never occurred to me. I was distressed sometimes, when I stopped to think about it, about Paul changing, about the lover and friend who had become a hard man. I was aware of the fact that he was fashioning a role for himself that did not agree with the way he used to be. Sometimes I felt fear when I tried to superimpose the contours of his current image onto the outlines of his former self, I felt fear at the many blurred edges. But not many of us manage to remain the way we were. We all change from within, besides adopting the protective coloring of our milieu: I had changed, too. Paul had a choice, and he chose to become what he became. And our love affair became a friendly bond, a tolerant familiarity with each other's shortcomings. That's what it had seemed to me, Helene thought.

———

AFTER THEIR RETURN from Switzerland, their apartment had become much too cramped for them, and they moved to a small town house not far from the campus. The small house had ivy rippling along its front and a fenced-in yard behind, with linden trees all around. Helene would collect the linden blossoms, filling the whole house with a familiar fragrance. Their neighbors had four small children, and Elizabeth made herself useful baby-sitting whenever Sally needed a free afternoon.

Helene felt very comfortable in the small house. She liked its Colonial design and began to be interested in American country antiques, trying to furnish the house in that cozy style. Paul wanted an Oriental rug for the living room, because he felt himself to be too successful to live like a poor man, he said jokingly. Helene thought of the family Orientals that she had stored in the Prague cellar, long ago, because they had seemed too middle-class to her. For a while the new purchase seemed like a capitulation, like a changeover to a dangerously sedate way of life. But then she found that the red Bukhara really went quite nicely with the pine cupboard. In wintertime, when there was a fire in the fireplace and the girls and their friends were popping corn, the

Oriental even turned out to be quite practical. It showed neither the spilled butter nor the lost unpopped corn kernels, which Agatha, the basset hound puppy, disdained.

But after a while Paul began to dislike the small town house. It was much too modest, he said; it looked more like a gazebo than a real, solid house. The neighborhood was becoming run-down, the street was noisy and dusty in the summer, he could not keep the windows of his study open because of the traffic.

"We are never here in the summer, anyway," Helene laughed. She was used to Paul's moods and took them lightly. "You really do sound like a dissatisfied housewife," she teased Paul. Then she became serious. "We have always moved every two or three years," she said. "I would like to stay somewhere, strike roots somewhere. Please."

She loved the small house, resisted giving it up for a long time. But Paul did not think their way of life appropriate to his status. No other professor lived in such shabby surroundings, he pointed out. They were no longer poor refugees, why should they live in a gazebo in the middle of a slum? Didn't he deserve better?

When the joking turned serious, Helene gave up and went to see real-estate agents. After three years in the small house, they moved again. From the very beginning the large white house in the suburbs did not appeal to her. It was much too impersonal. There were too many rooms, no cozy crannies, no turned staircases, no ivy rippling over the walls outside, no fragrant linden trees.

Paul was enthusiastic. "You can make it livable," he said. "You know how. Let me have my fun! I want to live better, I want to have some elegance!" He praised the fresh country air, the way the light would touch the tips of the trees every night before the sun went down. He ordered an expensive white couch for the living room and promised never to complain about the bus commute.

So Helene made the best of it. She took pains to arrange the house comfortably, saw to it that it became as pleasant to live in as the small town house had been. If it gives Paul so much pleasure, she thought, if he finds country life so much to his liking, then I will certainly not be the spoilsport. It is not often that he is so happy about something. It really is a beautiful house, the children love it here, and I will grow to like it, too. Haven't I always adapted to everything?

That summer there was a gypsy-moth blight in the suburbs. All the young green was eaten away, all the bushes were bare, as were many of the trees. Even the old elm in front of the white house showed bare spots. Standing still for a moment, one could hear the crunching of thousands of tiny jaws.

The upkeep, the cleaning, the simple task of running the large house took endless hours. Helene did not have much help. Cleaning ladies were unpredictable and demanding, and most of the time they were only willing to push the vacuum cleaner through the rooms. Sometimes they worked so devastatingly that a cleanup had to be done after them. During the first spring in the large white house, after a heavy downpour, there was a flood in the cellar. When the water had all been pumped out, the firemen discovered where it had originated: behind the house, an air-raid shelter had been sunk into the ground. When the water level began to rise, it over-flowed. The shelter had been built in the fifties, by people who had intended to survive a nuclear war in it.

Helene had a pump installed to regulate the water surplus. Outwardly, she would laugh about the foolish-ness of building a nuclear shelter that depended on electricity. But the nasty subterranean hole under their blooming paradise, and the wartime memories the shel-ter evoked, gave her nightmares. She could not talk to Paul about them.

Their relationship, in the routine of their daily existence, had begun to float. Like the couple in Edward Hopper's painting they moved, each of them alone, on the surface. Once in a while Helene would attempt to delve under the smooth ripples, would try to shake them both into recapturing, into expressing their thoughts about their predicament. Her attempts to break the sterility of their space usually ended in fond encounters in their bedroom. "This is not exactly what I meant," Helene would say afterward, in English, laughing at them both. "What I meant to ask was, why are you nice and funny only when you want to sleep with me?"

"Then I must be nice and funny all the time," Paul would answer, eyeing her with mock lecherousness. "We don't need to talk, do we? Look at you, forty-five years old, and you still expect romantic patter! That's not what an old marriage is about!"

"But I need to talk to you," Helene would whisper. "Listen to me—"

Paul would already be asleep, and Helene went back to her own empty space. We do communicate, she would comfort herself. Communication does not need to be filled with words at every stage. It is all right the way it is.

Paul did not permit himself much leisure to enjoy the beautiful house he had so coveted. He would wave to Helene from his third-floor study when she worked in the garden tending her bed of zinnias or sat at the garden table enjoying tea with one of her friends. Then he would go back to his desk. Helene wondered: Did he too feel the emptiness? Did he feel it up there? No, he seemed content, as long as the daily routine was undisturbed, as long as there were no demands made on his time.

He often went on lecture tours and consultation trips. He was a fascinating lecturer, and universities valued his visits whether as guest or adviser. He was paid extremely well. But all his additional income, all the royalties from his textbooks, all the lecture and consulting fees for which he gave up the little free time he had, they went into a separate bank account. Sometimes he would sit on Helene's yellow kitchen stool and would explain how much he intended to make on this article, how much was coming to him on that consultation, how much he would earn on that particular lecture tour. Then he would take off, go to the Caribbean and to South America, and would come back temporarily refreshed and exuberant, full of funny stories, his suitcase full of presents for the three of them. It pleased Helene that Paul still had the ability to unwind. She wasn't upset about his separate vacations: it was impossible for her to go with him; there was no one to take care of the children for a long enough stretch of time. To engage a babysitter for several weeks would make a trip much too expensive, it took too much of Paul's salary just to run the house. Besides, going by himself seemed to be to Paul's taste, and she did not find that strange. She felt concern for him and guessed that at this point in life he needed and cherished solitude after all the pressures. Didn't she herself also enjoy the relaxed days of his absences?

"Of course I miss him," she would tell her friends. "But a vacation from each other is beneficial for a marriage. Just try it!"

———

W<small>HEN</small> B<small>ERNARD AND I DECIDED</small> that we had lived in Cambridge long enough, that it was time to change the scene, I didn't know about the American Bethlehem. Bernard spoke of the robust Pennsylvania manner, as opposed to the tight-lipped understated New England way. He clearly was eager to get back to the former. He mentioned Bethlehem. Bethlehem?

Yes, I knew of Bethlehem Steel: the pylons and T-beams destined to support the Lisbon Bridge had, twenty years before, all borne that inscription. When I saw the Bethlehem plant they had come from, the memory of the bittersweet summer surfaced, floated past, the way happy white clouds float past on a fragrant summer day.

I also knew that Hilda Doolittle, the poet H.D., whose letters we had transcribed and translated one winter a long time ago, had grown up on Bethlehem's Church Street. But it was the gentle hills surrounding the town that convinced me that I wanted to settle there. For me, too, those hills were like the hills of eastern Moravia, where I had spent the first ten years of my life.

———

WHEN AT LONG LAST the girls became old enough to be left overnight or even for a weekend, Helene could accompany Paul on lecture trips, if they did not involve going too far. Paul liked her to drive him from one place to another. And she enjoyed the respect that was shown him everywhere. She had always admired him for his honesty, for his willingness to tell the truth as he saw it. Now she began to admire his courage to face unpopular issues, to take a stand on them. It was the time of the Vietnam War, uncertainty and disillusionment came from all directions. Authority was being challenged and questioned everywhere. Watergate was like a spreading, festering sore. America, which to them had always stood for absolute and unquestioned good, was no longer without blemish.

And Paul, although deeply disappointed himself, met the students' questioning and challenges. She was very proud of him in these moments, happy with the attentive faces of the young people, the charismatic effect he had on them, the silence whenever he spoke, the applause that very often turned into a standing ovation. It was all worth it, she thought in these moments, pleased with the small reflection of his fame that shone on her.

But she was far from feeling like a wallflower: her second book, the one about her family, had been published in Germany and was praised and discussed by the reviewers. The royalties she received she spent at once and with great enthusiasm: on a pine cupboard for the kitchen, on a painting by an artist of the Hudson River School, a captain's chest, a large pink azalea bush to plant in front of the white house, a row of junipers to fence in the backyard. Sometimes Paul would joke that she was earning more with her two books than he himself with all his degrees and lecture and consultation fees. It was not quite true, but they laughed about it often, and after a time it became a family joke.

They would exchange views and advise each other on their efforts. Helene knew her limitations and followed Paul's suggestions in matters of style. Paul on the other hand valued Helene's common sense. She was often able to dilute a sentence of his that was too complex, a passage that seemed to her to be too crowded with literary jargon. Their minds were different, but in balance. They were able to follow each other's thoughts without too many words. There was a confidence and an intimacy between them that only a life spent together can produce. They dedicated their books to each other.

Elizabeth was almost eighteen. In winter she had spent hours filling out college applications, and now she had chosen to go to Columbia. It had been her first choice, and the fact that she was accepted brought great rejoicing.

In early September Helene and Paul drove her to New York. Paul went more or less against his will, because the trip meant a loss of two working days for him. But, for the first time in their married life, Helene had insisted. He just would have to come this time, she said. To be taken to college by one's parents, that was a once-in-a-lifetime experience, an American tradition, and Elizabeth should not be deprived of it. Paul would simply have to postpone his work two days. Paul, in mock exasperation, relented. "Your mother is becoming very assertive," he told Elizabeth.

Elizabeth sat in the backseat of the old Peugeot, squeezed between her bags, books and records and ice skates, and wept all the way to New York. Each of her friends was leaving for a different school, her youth was over, she sobbed. She would be a college student now, responsible for herself—

At night, after they had deposited the again cheerful Elizabeth and her belongings at the dorm, Helene and

Paul sat at the hotel bar, looking at the Manhattan skyline. They enjoyed their gin fizzes after the day's upheavals, and were amazed at how fast the years had gone by. "It seems just yesterday that I took her to elementary school for the first time," Helene mused.

"Now we really belong to the older generation," Paul noted with horror. "In another while we'll be grandparents!"

But later, in their room above Central Park, they made certain that the years had not diminished their enthusiasm for each other.

———

AFTER CHRISTMAS VACATION, that winter after Paul's departure, the principal of Margaret's junior high school called Helene to his office. "There have been several complaints about Margaret's behavior," he said, "and it would be good to examine the matter immediately."

Helene was worried: never before had anybody complained about the behavior of her girls. They were rambunctious, yes, but never behavior problems. She watched with apprehension as they entered the conference room one after the other, the math teacher, the history teacher, the chemistry teacher, the two teachers for French and English.

"Margaret is insolent and rude in my class," the history teacher said, frowning. "I've had to warn her three times since last fall."

The math teacher nodded in agreement. "She is disruptive, does not accomplish what she should, never does."

"Most distracted during experiments," the chemistry teacher added. "So much that she has not finished a single assignment this last quarter. She'll fail the year if she continues this way."

All three were in complete agreement. All three men of about fifty, well-intentioned, experienced with adolescents. The two women teachers had looked puzzled for a while. They looked at each other. The English teacher, a young woman, shook her head. "Are we talking about Margaret in seventh grade?" she asked.

"Of course we are," said the principal, looking surprised.

"I was just going to ask the same question," said the French teacher, an older woman. "I have the feeling that we are discussing two different students here. There can be no question that Margaret is an A student."

"That's exactly what I mean." The English teacher was quite emphatic. "Margaret is quiet, maybe a bit too much so, but always well prepared, helpful in my class. There can be absolutely no question of her being insolent or disruptive!"

"The best student in my French class," the older woman added.

The principal looked at each of the teachers in turn,

baffled. Then he turned to Helene, winked, and tried a joke. "Could it be that Margaret—hates men?" He laughed, whinnied, proud of his deduction.

Everyone laughed at the notion, politely.

Helene haltingly explained the probable reason for Margaret's probable dislike of men, explained Paul's decision to leave. They all stopped laughing and looked embarrassed. They nodded with understanding, came close to apologies; yes, there is so much of this going on right now, it is lamentable. They promised to be especially considerate, they were kind and decent people who meant well.

Nevertheless, Helene sat in the car afterward, bawling like a child. Because they had been so kind and had meant so well and because, yes, there was so much of this going on right now. We are becoming a statistic, she thought. And we were always so proud of ourselves, for being special, for being outstanding.

———

WE DID GO TO ICHENHAUSEN ONE SUMMER, Bernard and I. We knew, of course, that it would be very unlike my pilgrimage to the town of my grandparents, in 1945, where the house on Prague Street, although hardly recognizable, was still very much there, the garden gate guarded by the two silver firs. After all, Bernard's

connection to Ichenhausen was going back five generations. There would be no memories, no links to hold onto,
no sudden recollections of place. And still, as we approached along the country road lined with poplars and
later stood on the town's square, in front of the house
that still bears his family's name, there was, for Bernard,
a familiarity. Because he could not see the modern
housefronts, he could imagine much better than I could
how things must have been when his great-great-
grandfather lived there. In the cemetery he could make
out, with sensitive blind man's fingertips, the weathered
Hebrew inscriptions much better than I did with my
eyes. Many of the gravestones, overgrown with moss
and lichen, bore his family's name. And in the small
synagogue that miraculously survived by serving the
Nazis as a grain depot, where the present Bavarian
government had established a museum, in many photographs and documents collected from the region, Bernard's family name is repeated, many times, like in a
mirror image.

———

*T*HAT LAST YEAR OF THEIR MARRIAGE was the
year of Paul's sabbatical. After they had brought Elizabeth to college, Paul, who didn't need to work in Europe
for a whole year, decided that he would only go for short

trips. He would spend three months in London in the fall, them come back to Cambridge, then do more research in England and on the continent in the spring. "I'm getting set in my ways," he said. "I like my own study to work in best of all." Helene was staying home with Margaret, teaching her college course. Elizabeth's freshman-year expenses would be high. They would need her salary.

Shortly before Christmas Paul came back from London as planned, cheerful as ever after a trip, with presents for each of them, which showed care and thoughtfulness. He was satisfied with the work he had done in the British Museum in those three months; the time had been a productive period for him. They were happy to be together again. Elizabeth had survived her first semester with great aplomb. Everything was going well for all of them.

For the spring, Paul and Helene were planning a trip alone together. Olga and Joseph, although busy with their own family, had offered to take Margaret for two weeks, and Helene felt that the girl at eleven and a half, was old enough not to be any trouble.

They had wanted to go to Greece for many years. But as they began to pore over guidebooks and brochures, it became obvious that the two weeks of Helene's spring recess would not be enough to see everything they wanted to see. "We can go to Greece in another year or two," Paul decided. "When we have more time on our hands. Now we ought to look at somewhere closer."

Since Paul was going to England, anyway, they

ordered tickets for London. And it was a good choice: London, in March, was full of spring. Even the window boxes at Buckingham Palace were overflowing with tulips and daffodils. The theaters were a never-ending pleasure, every night. There were old friends to see and several elderly cousins, twice or three times removed, whose afternoon teas Paul attended under protest. But Helene was intrigued by the thought that people still existed to whom she was related, who were family, even in the most distant way. And they made plans for Paul's lecture tour in the spring of the following year. They would take Margaret, too, and rent a car for a trip through the English countryside, which they did not yet know.

At an antiques stall on the Portobello Road Paul discovered a glass paperweight with thousands of little flowers forming the inscription Home Sweet Home. He insisted on buying it for his desk, although Helene laughed and found it much too camp for her own taste.

In the Imperial War Museum they were moved by the flimsy planes and makeshift shelters of the Battle of Britain, and by the change that had since taken place in the shape of machines. Even the Sherman tank that had won the war, that had made such an impression on them in their refugee days, was now a museum piece. It made them remember how long they had been friends, how many different lives they had lived together in the course of the many years.

Once, during dinner at the Swiss Restaurant in Piccadilly Circus, they both leaned back and said, looking at each other, "We really are living it up, aren't we?"

"Are you content with your life, all in all?" Helene asked.

"Do I look as if I weren't?" Paul answered.

Helene leaned forward across the dish with carrot salad and kissed him.

"Be careful," Paul said. "Old people don't do such things in England!"

They both giggled like conspirators.

After twelve days they parted. Helene went back home to Margaret and to teaching. Paul stayed in London, where he wanted to continue preparing a new course for next fall.

But two weeks later he telephoned. He was ill, he had had terrible stomach pains, and the London doctor had mentioned a possible liver ailment, possible complications. He wanted to come home on the next plane. Would Helene contact his doctor and make an appointment immediately for a thorough checkup?

When she picked Paul up at Kennedy Airport the following day, he was pale and depressed, spoke about feeling old, used up. But his doctor, after a thorough examination, found him entirely well. The pains could have been due to a mild food poisoning, he theorized, from which Paul had now completely recovered. There was no reason to worry whatsoever.

After several days, Paul perked up again. He began to laugh about the scare the London doctor had given him. On a beautiful morning in May, when the apple tree in the backyard was sending a glow like freshly fallen snow through the entire house, Paul once again was shouting and angrily throwing his books around, because Helene had forgotten to pick up his suit at the cleaner's. He is feeling his old self again, she thought wryly, and breathed a sigh of relief.

Then he furiously rushed down the stairs and fell, ripping pictures off the wall in falling, sending his briefcase flying through the air. There he lay on the hallway rug, pale, the back of his head bleeding. In falling, he had hit the banister. Helene ran to get a wet towel, Margaret ordered Paul to stretch out and not move, and Elizabeth rushed to the liquor cabinet to pour a glass of bourbon. Paul refused it with a weak smile, and the girl drank it herself in her confusion, shaking, almost as pale as her father.

It took several stitches to repair the damage. The small shaved spot on the back of Paul's head was not quite grown over yet, the frightening moments were not yet quite forgotten, the broken pictures not yet repaired. Then Paul informed Helene one day that Nell was in town. "We have to invite her for dinner," he said.

"Really?" Helene said. "What is she doing here?"

Paul and Nell, she knew, had encountered each other at conventions and meetings quite often. Years ago Paul had told her that Nell had divorced and remarried. At that time Helene had asked, "Are you having an affair with her again?" And Paul had turned up his eyes and had said no, of course not: Nell had grown staid and chubby since their Columbia days. Now the memory came back to Helene, of the sand, of the earrings between the car upholstery, of the hot lonely Sundays on Gilgo Beach. She shuddered.

"She is a visiting member of a committee," Paul explained. "Poor woman, she has totally lost her looks. We should invite some people, make her feel at home. You can cook—"

"No," Helene said slowly. "Nell will not set foot in my house."

"Excuse me?" Paul said, surprised.

"I am not going to cook for Nell," said Helene. She was surprised at her own vehemence.

Paul shrugged. That is your problem, his shrug told her. If you want to be difficult—

She waited for Paul to say something more, to suggest an alternative she could agree to, to suggest that they could both take Nell to a restaurant, to a college dining room. Paul remained silent, did not mention the matter again. But several days later Helene saw him having lunch at the faculty club, with Nell.

She felt angry and humiliated. This is how it is, she thought, this is how it has always been. Paul, in motion, and I, burdened forever with memories, our history, everyone's history. But I am no longer the girl I once was. I am no longer willing to be passive, the way I once was. I am somebody, too. I want to be considered.

That summer Elizabeth was especially difficult. She had a hard time adjusting to life at home after one year's independence at school. She expected to be waited on when she came home from her summer job. She let Helene feel her annoyance in a manner similar to Paul's, and was snappy the way nineteen-year-old daughters sometimes are with their mothers when family life is not to their liking. And Paul, instead of admonishing Elizabeth, instead of reminding her of her limits, pretended not to hear. Sometimes he would take Elizabeth's side, would be sarcastic with Helene, sounding not at all like the father of the family, but like someone much closer to the girls in age and attitude. Once she found him rummaging in Elizabeth's desk. She was surprised at his lack of respect for his daughter's privacy. After he discovered several letters from young men, he seemed perturbed. He would lie on the couch in his study for hours, away from everybody, brooding.

Helene had too much to do that last summer. She had agreed to teach a summer course every morning. Margaret had broken her wrist and had to be taken to the hospital for X rays, twice a week. Elizabeth, sensing tension, demanded more and more attention. Paul insisted, as always, on a three-course dinner at precisely six o'clock. The large white house and its eternal upkeep hounded Helene. She felt cornered. Her recurring dream plagued her: she would wake up from it, shaking with fright, exhausted from trying to hide her nakedness so that no one would see. What is it that I cannot let anyone find out? she would ask herself again and again.

---

*M*EMORY, THE ABILITY TO REMEMBER, is the most elusive of all human faculties. Scientists today assume that it is not a set of fixed records, but a constantly evolving shifting process among different locations in the brain. Memory loss is therefore an extremely subtle development, which can remain undetected for many years.

---

*L*ATE AT NIGHT, when he finished his day's work, Paul would take the dog for a walk: he called it their constitutional. After ten o'clock Agatha became restless and would waddle up to the third floor. She would lie in front of Paul's study, with her long basset hound ears daintily spread on the floor, waiting. When Paul put down his pen or pushed the typewriter aside, she would stand up and be ready, smiling, wagging her behind. After their walk Paul would lock the house for the night by pulling the latch.

The first time that Paul locked the house in this

manner without Helene's being home, she found it funny and laughed about his professorial absentmindedness. She had to throw pebbles against the bedroom window. Ringing and knocking would have awakened the girls and also started Agatha howling. She had not wanted to call out, because she would have been embarrassed at their neighbors hearing her.

The second time it happened she still joked about it. "Is this a Freudian slip?" she asked. "Didn't you notice that I kissed you good night before I left for the library?"

The third time she became angry. She slammed the door after Paul had opened it for her, not caring whether anyone heard. Paul sighed. He was appalled because she had awakened him. He had to teach early next morning.

When she had to spend part of the night sitting in the garden, that last summer, because no pebbles and no knocking had helped, she shouted. Was it all the same to him? Didn't he notice whether she was home or not?

"I don't know what you are yelling about," Paul said. "This can happen to anyone! You're inside now, aren't you?"

She did not answer but began to cry, not knowing herself why, at the time. Only days later did the memory suddenly surface: when she was fifteen, in Prague, and her mother had just died, her father had also locked her out one Sunday afternoon. He had had a woman in their apartment. The memory: hot and full of anguish, Helene's fury, the neighbor who opened the door across the hall and tried to calm her down. And then her father, who finally opened the door, his eyes red rimmed—

She did not explain her tears to Paul anymore. That

summer, with her mouth set, she unscrewed the latch and removed it.

Something had happened to Helene in the course of that last summer. She did not have much time to think about it, but even if she had had the time, she would not have been able to put it into words. The feeling of anger and humiliation she had felt on seeing Paul and Nell at the faculty club kept surfacing. And the memory of herself, locked out of the house so many times, suddenly made her see what she had not wanted to see for a long time: that she was, in the same way, locked out of Paul's life. This brought a change over her; she no longer sang and laughed. She no longer asked friendly questions, no longer smoothed things over, no longer made sure that everyone was content at all times. She withdrew every night, exhausted at the thought of the next day.

And suddenly, everything looked different. Suddenly, there was no more warmth, no good-night kisses, no jokes over the breakfast table, no quick hug in passing, no affirmation of a friendly presence. The girls, suddenly unsure, did not comment. But she wondered again and again: would it have been like this between Paul and me, years ago, if I had not made all the efforts? If I could do it over again, would I behave in the same way? Would I make the same decisions? And, if I had acted differently, what difference would it have made?

She saw now that all the warmth, all the personal touches of daily life had been provided only by her for a long time. When she gave up providing them, only tense politeness remained. Within this field of politeness

Helene and Paul moved, like two chess figures, slowly but inevitably toward the decisive confrontation.

———

BERNARD, HAPPY AND CHEERFUL even before his morning coffee, sings in the shower. Songs about sad lovers are not in his repertory. He sings, without quite holding the tune, songs that were popular before my time in America, "Don't sit under the apple tree," and "If a body meets a body coming through the rye."

He tells me of a long succession of live-in maids and couples who used to sing in the kitchen when he was growing up: first the Irish and then the Germans, who took him to church every Sunday and, later, the black woman, Minnie, who made the best apple pies he ever ate. From college, he would send his laundry home every week in a metal container. When the container came back, it would hold, beside the clean laundry, Minnie's apple pie. Bernard's fraternity brothers always managed to be around when Minnie's laundry box arrived from Philadelphia.

When Bernard wanted to show me his alma mater in the middle of Pennsylvania, we drove through a town called Lititz. This town—whose core and main employer now is a chocolate factory that for years used to supply Bernard's family plant with cocoa—was also founded by

Moravian Brethren. The sign on the town square says that they named it after a village in Bohemia that had sheltered them, in the eighteenth century, from the wrath of the Catholic Church. Two centuries later the very same Bohemian village was destroyed by the Nazis as a reprisal, for its inhabitants had again given shelter to "enemies."

In the first months after the war, when I lived in the studio overlooking the Weinberg section, I earned my living by coloring prints of that Bohemian village, the village of Lidice. People were then buying the prints— either to express their happiness at having survived or to assuage their guilt at having survived—like hotcakes.

———

IN MAY, THE LARGE WHITE HOUSE in the suburbs was sold to a young couple with three children. The For Sale sign under the elm was covered with a red paper strip that said Sold. Helene and Margaret sat staring at it all evening, unable to speak to each other. Then the girl went out into the garden. The apple tree was blooming there like never before, displaying its glow to them for the last time. Margaret worked on its trunk for an hour, in the gleam of her flashlight, her teeth clenched. When she finished, she showed Helene the carving. "Margaret and Elizabeth lived here," it said.

"So those three brats won't ever forget it," she said, her lower lip quivering.

Then Helene went hunting for a less expensive place to live, taking Margaret along. Margaret, at thirteen, very serious and with a grown-up expression, voiced her opinions: she knew exactly what she liked and disliked, how they should live together in the future. They found a town house with a tiny garden in a nicely landscaped area, with one bedroom for each of them and a spare one for Elizabeth. Helene's half from the proceeds of the sale of the large house would be just enough to pay for it. They were both pleased with their success.

Paul had moved to campus, to a residence for graduate students. Soon Margaret reported that he had gone to England for the planned lecture series. The previous March, when they were in London together, Paul had arranged for the tour. They had studied the itinerary, and they had agreed to rent a car and go on side trips to castles and cathedrals between the lectures. It was to be a leisurely family trip, with Margaret in the backseat and with Helene hopefully mastering the art of driving in the wrong lane. At last, Helene thought, at last we would have had the peace to enjoy such a journey. Always before, with two lively children in the back, it had been a matter of getting from one place to the next, as quickly as possible. The most beautiful Romanesque church thus became reduced, for the children's sake, to a memory of a rooster crowing or a cat to be petted in front of it. Now, when the girls are old enough—

She tried to fight back the anger that threatened to

surface whenever she imagined Paul on his solitary journey. But then, he might not be alone, Paul, so handsome, almost unchanged, except for a few wrinkles around his eyes. Even when we're old, he had said, I'll always come back to you. And I have always forgiven him, she thought. But I will never be able to forgive him for lying to himself, for lying to himself about us, for forgetting about our history.

But then Helene stopped herself, went to her room, to her desk, to her translation. Ten years from now, there will have to be more left over from this year than anger and sadness. On her desk there were the two volumes she had written. She touched them with a flash of pride. When I finish translating, she thought, then there will be three.

But still, the sadness was often more than she could bear. When the past came crawling out of drawers and closets ready to be packed, staring Helene in the face. The bookshelf they had bought in Munich, their first antique purchase, the ship's lantern from Maine, the cheerfully orange and yellow *Mother and Child* by Chagall, bought the summer before Elizabeth's birth. The glass paperweight from the Portobello Road, the one with thousands of little flowers forming the inscription Home Sweet Home. Their family past was being loaded into the moving van.

The new town house was clean and friendly. Helene filled it with the things she had liked best in the large white house: the pine cupboard, the captain's chest, the white couch. Her small collection of primitive paintings looked good on the white living room walls. This time, the Oriental did not go into the cellar. It held too many memories of children growing up. It belonged in the living room.

A few days after moving in, when she had succeeded in organizing the chaos, she stopped for a look around her. She stood again, just like thirty-two years ago in Prague, on her own. There was no "Manhattan skyline" outside her window now, but a landscaped park with spruces and forsythia bushes. The kitchen window framed a dogwood tree. There were no clues to her former existence outside, no large white house to remind her of failure, of the second home she had lost.

Relief once again came from other women. Helene's friends came and admired the town house, bringing presents and cakes and flowers to celebrate. From a nursery, a baby silver fir tree was delivered one day and planted in front of the living room window. Claire had it sent from Montreal. *For you to grow with you*, she had written inside a card that said "Congratulations!"

Helene finished her translation according to her self-imposed schedule, and sent it to a New York publisher. Margaret, pride about having started it all exuding from her like a halo, was again bringing home A's in math and science. And Helene knew that she was much richer now than thirty-two years ago: she had two daughters, she had a family. She had friends, and maybe there would be someone one day, someone she hadn't even met yet. She was not alone the way she had been in those postwar months.

She felt younger and more alive than she had felt in years. I'm managing all right, her appearance signaled, I have not been drowned by the breaking wave, the white foam, Gilgo Beach. I have surfaced. Her recurring dream, the one of trying to escape before being found out, never returned.

———

*T*HE GENTLE HILLS SURROUNDING THE TOWN of Bethlehem, then, became our home, Bernard's and mine. From the windows of our house I can see the river, blinking among the trees, and behind it the green cupola of the Moravian church. During the night we hear the whistles of the freight trains, as they cross the iron bridge on their way to the Bethlehem Steel plant. Going, their rumbling is hollow, for the wagons are empty. Coming back, there is a different sound to them, a heaviness, which Bernard, with his sensitive hearing, taught me to distinguish.

The old Moravian cemetery in the old part of town, where the gravestones are lying flat, facing the sky, is my favorite place in Bethlehem. Many of the names on the stones are Czech names, many of the Brethren and Sisters buried there were born either in Moravia or in Saxony. I like to think of them coming here, at long last free to live according to their truth, being kind to the heathens they found, industrious and inventive. In the Moravian Archives there are portraits of many of them. Their faces are cheerful, unlined, as if the women in their white bonnets all had known about cold mountain streams with magic powers. Their portraits hang next to a portrait of Comenius, next to the bust of Jan Hus. Portraits of Comenius, the teacher and humanist who was an exile and who was asked to teach in America, hung in all the Czech schools I ever attended. Jan Hus, who demanded truth as they burned him at the stake, was in all the history textbooks I ever studied. The leather-bound folios with their illuminated texts, which I found in the air-conditioned vaults of the Moravian Archives, are all written in medieval Czech.

Hilda Doolittle's house on Church Street no longer exists. It has given way to a modern glass-and-steel building of the town library. Perhaps H.D., who turned her back on Bethlehem early in her life, to float nervously from place to place, demanding help from Sigmund Freud in many letters I know almost by heart, would relent and approve of it. I do. I like to volunteer my services there.

The Bethlehem star in many doorways in town is of an entirely different shape than the castle named Star, by which Gerd and I walked in the suburbs of Prague, on White Mountain, a whole lifetime ago. Walking with Bernard, I describe to him the river as it flows between the hills. It is different from the cold mountain brook of the folk song I sang when I was young. But nothing is ever lost: even in it I see a connection, a circle that closed. It is one of the many circles that form a life, some of which we comprehend, and some of which we never will.